AFTER
ABSALON

SIMON OKOTIE

SALT

CROMER

PUBLISHED BY SALT PUBLISHING 2020

2 4 6 8 10 9 7 5 3 1

First published in Great Britain in 2020 by
Salt Publishing Ltd
12 Norwich Road, Cromer NR27 0AX United Kingdom

www.saltpublishing.com

Salt Publishing Limited Reg. No. 5293401

A CIP catalogue record for this book is available from the British Library

ISBN 978 1 78463 166 6 (Paperback edition)
ISBN 978 1 78463 167 3 (Electronic edition)

Typeset in Neacademia by Salt Publishing

Printed and bound in Great Britain by Clays Ltd, Elcograf S.p.A

SIMON OKOTIE was born to Nigerian/
English parents. He lives in London.

For
Sanghasiha

AFTER ABSALON

1

T HE RAMP LED down from the flat area of pavement or sidewalk across which Marguerite was moving and then turned back on itself, via a horizontal rectangular plane, before descending, at precisely, he thought, the same gradient into the pedestrian underpass proper. And the function of the horizontal rectangular plane was to provide the landing position, as it were, not only for the ramp down which Marguerite would imminently descend, but also for a flight of stairs towards which a woman in a tight-fitting pinstriped suit was headed, as it's known. Note, though, that the precise landing positions of the two protagonists, to call them that, would not be at the same location upon this horizontal rectangular plane, presumably for reasons of safety: when viewed from above, the end of the ramp furthest from Marguerite formed the left half of the rectangle's closest long side whilst the edge of the top step formed the top half of the short side furthest from him, such that the landing position of the woman in the tight-fitting pinstriped suit would, according to Marguerite's rapid mental deliberations, be in the left half of the top-right quadrant of that horizontal rectangular plane (given that the steps extended and descended from right to left across that quadrant), whereas Marguerite himself would land in the bottom half of the bottom-left quadrant of the plane since it was this quadrant that intersected, at its bottom edge, the ramp that extended and descended from pavement or sidewalk level directly in front of him. In other words, the long, flat, sloping rectangle that was the ramp down from ground level joined the horizontal rectangular plane that was arranged at right angles to it (and to the ramp down to the mouth of the pedestrian underpass proper), with this horizontal rectangular plane (which was located halfway, or thereabouts, between ground- and subway-level) also being joined, as it were, in the opposite half from its intersection with the slope down from ground-level, by a series of much smaller, parallel (or should that be contiguous?), horizontal rectangles of decreasing (or increasing, depending where you were – or are – situated) altitude and of decreasing (or increasing, as before) distance from that intersection, with the decreasing (etc.) altitude being regulated by a further series of parallel or contiguous rectangles of the same (or similar) size (to each other) but arranged vertically at decreasing (etc.) distance from that intersection such that the two sets of smaller rectangles intersected (or were, in fact, fabricated in situ, as a block) to form a step-wise arrangement that joined the aforementioned horizontal rectangular plane whose breadth was twice the width of each of the ramps leading initially away from, and then back down towards, the mouth of the pedestrian underpass proper; and the reason the ramp down from the sidewalk did not terminate in the same half of the horizontal rectangular plane as the steps, and that the orientation of the steps was at right angles to the ramp down to the mouth of the pedestrian underpass proper, related quite straightforwardly, Marguerite thought, as his right foot touched down at the top of the ramp, to the following interrelated safety concerns: were someone such as a cyclist or roller-skater to freewheel, no doubt in contravention of local by-laws, down the ramp from pavement level, they would risk colliding with anyone descending the steps onto the horizontal rectangular plane were those steps to be located in the same half of that plane as the ramp; similarly were the steps to be aligned with, rather than at right angles to, the ramp down from the horizontal rectangular plane to the mouth of the pedestrian underpass proper then a skateboarder, say, might be tempted, again no doubt in contravention of local by-laws, to jump the steps straight onto that ramp, thereby endangering anyone using that ramp to move towards or away from the pedestrian underpass proper that spanned that broad tree-lined avenue with a row of showrooms on one side of it and a wide expanse of parkland on the other. It was for these reasons, then, that Marguerite's landing position, were he to continue down the ramp and onto that horizontal rectangular plane, would be different to that of the woman in the tight-fitting pinstriped suit, or, more specifically, the landing position of his feet, or the soles of his shoes, were he to be wearing shoes (broadly defined), would be different to that – or those (etc.) – of the woman in the tight-fitting pinstriped suit, for the reasons previously adumbrated, this all being predicated upon Marguerite actually continuing down the ramp in question towards the horizontal rectangular plane en route to the pedestrian underpass proper, which he now committed fully to doing by lifting his left foot from the sidewalk in what was presumably a parabola – the upward arc of same, that is, which would, in fact, terminate at a lower level (and, hence, at a slightly more advanced position than otherwise) than that of its launching point, given that it would have joined (or, in fact, surpassed, as it were) the right foot which was already on the ramp leading down to, yet away, for now, from, the mouth of the pedestrian underpass proper that crossed underneath the broad, tree-lined avenue that he had his back, and, indeed, the other parts of the rear of his body, to, with the reason for proceeding in this manner being what he took to be a mutual physical attraction to the woman in the tight-fitting pinstriped suit, as his opposite (meaning that they tended, all else being equal, towards each other, as bodies in space), as well as a sense that she would assist him in his investigation into the disappearance of Harold Absalon, the Mayor's transport advisor, who was missing presumed dead, although for now, she looked distinctly displeased to see him.

2

A FURTHER DIFFERENCE between him and the woman in the tight-fitting pinstriped suit – a difference, that is, in addition to the non-coincidence of their landing positions upon the horizontal rectangular plane – related to the *orientation* of their feet, his in his battered working man's boots, say, hers in her stylish working woman's shoes: whereas his front foot, having attained the surface of the ramp leading down to the horizontal rectangular plane, was now placed at an angle of minus whatever to the horizontal, with the 'whatever' relating to whatever the highway or wider transport authority deemed to be a suitable gradient for the situation that he and others using that ramp to descend to the horizontal rectangular plane found themselves in, her front foot would stay at zero degrees to the horizontal plane formed by the top step, which is to say that it would not subtend any angle, whether positive or negative, to the horizontal, regardless of the angle that it decided, as it were, to subtend between its launch point at the top of that flight of stairs and its landing position one step down from that launch point. That, then, was a further difference between them, Marguerite thought, as he noticed that the woman in the tight-fitting pinstriped suit had turned right towards the steps and, in so doing, confirmed Marguerite's suspicion that she was holding a briefcase in her right hand belonging to Richard Knox, an influential colleague of Harold Absalon with whom the Mayor's transport advisor had fallen out, as it's known, shortly before his disappearance.[1]

On further reflection, however, he realised that the feet of the woman in the tight-fitting pinstriped suit would, in fact, given that they were housed, as it were, in what are known as high-heeled shoes, be likely to remain at an angle (and he left unspecified, for now, whether the angle subtended by same was a negative or positive one in relation to the horizontal) given the elevation provided by those heels compared to the toes of the same pair of shoes. He had been wrong, in other words, to assert that unlike his front foot (which had, of course, attained the surface of the ramp leading down to the horizontal rectangular plane), the front foot of the woman in the tight-fitting pinstriped suit, on attaining the first step down the stairway to that horizontal rectangular plane, would remain at zero degrees to the horizontal, and that this was a further difference between him and that woman, or rather between their respective front feet – a difference additional, that is, to the non-coincidence of their landing points upon that plane. And the reason he had indicated this whilst now understanding that he had been wrong to have done so related to the inherent nature of the aforementioned high-heeled shoes that formed, he now realised, such a key part of the woman in the pinstriped suit's tight-fitting outfit, to call it that, a nature that was inherent, that is, in both what they were and what they were called, in that the heels of same were high, or, rather, that the heels of same were long such that, when one

1 It would seem, in fact, now that the project had entered what's known as its construction phase, that Knox had simply been spending his time on site overseeing operations there. I saw a photo of him with the Chancellor, it might have been, and other dignitaries during the ground-breaking ceremony, and felt intense irritation that it was him, rather than me, who was mixing in such circles.

(such as the woman in the tight-fitting pinstriped suit) was wearing them then, to the extent that they were being worn in the correct fashion, which is to say, the right way around, the heels of that person, which is to say, the heels of the person wearing those high-heeled shoes, would, and even will, be at an elevated position not only in relation to the toes (and, granted, the balls of the feet) of the same person but also in relation to the immediate area of the plane (assuming it to be solid) upon which the heels of those shoes were, as it were, resting, and, given this fact, which is to say the fact of the angle of the feet of the person wearing those high-heeled shoes – which is to say the woman in the tight-fitting pinstriped suit in the current scenario – then those feet would not, in fact, given the parameters inherent in the wearing of such footwear, be at zero degrees to the horizontal – unless, of course, she were walking up a ramp of precisely the same gradient (albeit in inverse) as the shoes in question (a tantalising prospect for Marguerite).

Were, then, the woman in the tight-fitting pinstriped suit to descend to the horizontal rectangular plane via the steps leading laterally down to it, a plane, remember, that also intersected the ramp leading down from the flat area of pavement or sidewalk across which Marguerite had latterly moved, and the ramp down to the pedestrian underpass that crossed beneath the broad tree-lined avenue roughly at right angles to it, the front (and, in time, in turn, the back) foot of that attractive woman would *not*, in fact, despite the fact that it would have launched itself from a flat, horizontal plane and would, in its descent, land upon a number (unspecified) of flat, horizontal planes at a steadily, although incrementally, decreasing altitude, necessarily be at a different angle to the feet of Marguerite, to call them that, even though his descent would have been made possible by his moving down a ramp which, by definition, was not at zero degrees to the horizontal, and the reason for this related, in summary, to the design of the high-heeled shoes that the woman in the pinstriped suit was wearing (and not, of course, just to the design of those specific shoes but to the design of all high-heeled shoes qua high-heeled shoes), a design that was to Marguerite's mind well captured, as it were, by the name of that item, or those items, viz 'high-heeled shoes'.

3

I N SAYING THAT his left foot, having left the level, in more
ways than one, of the pavement or sidewalk to commence the
upwards arc of what Marguerite presumed, in the absence of
his textbooks, to be a parabola, and, having attained the zenith
of that arc, had commenced its descent, would, as it were,
join the right, and would, in fact, land in advance of the latter
on the downward slope that initially led away from, but, in a
sense, would ultimately terminate at, the mouth of the pedestrian underpass proper, he wondered, in retrospect, whether,
in fact, the arc this parabola traced would be quite so pure,
geometrically speaking, as he was perhaps implying. What he
meant to say by this, as his left foot, in reality (whatever that
may mean in the circumstances in which we find ourselves in
in relation to him), passed his right foot, which is to say that
a projection vertically downwards from the centre-point of
his left foot passed a projection horizontally leftwards from
the centre-point of his right foot (rather than saying that a
projection vertically downwards from the rearmost point of his
left foot (the heel) passed a projection horizontally leftwards
from the foremost point of his right foot (the big toe, or, in
some subjects, the second toe from the right)), was that, in
saying that his left foot would trace this parabola and land at
a lower level than the right, that it would, for that reason, land
further in advance of the right than it would otherwise have
done, and that perhaps those two statements (and he would, of

course, come back to which two) were, in fact, incompatible, which is to say that he wondered whether he would, as his left foot commenced its downwards arc, the commencement of which coincided, more or less, with the moment at which that foot passed the right in the manner previously defined, be able to complete the beautiful parabolic sweep[2] that he was tracing with his left foot, or whether, given that the ground was, as it were, falling away, he would have to arrest this sweep prematurely, thereby adversely affecting the fine (and, note, symmetrical) lines that would, presumably, have been traced were he to have been walking, as it were, on the flat.

The answer to this conundrum would come soon enough, he knew, since his left foot would imminently complete the arc whose termination point was in advance of, and slightly below, his right foot. And what he noticed, as his left foot entered the earliest phase of this landing sequence, was that, rather than remaining roughly at right angles to the pavement/sidewalk from which he was advancing, his body (the rest of it) was, in fact, starting to lean forwards (from his perspective) such that, at the moment when his left foot (the ball, presumably, initially, thereof) touched down upon the slope leading initially away from, before turning back towards, the mouth, to continue calling it that, of the pedestrian underpass proper, in what's known as a dog-leg (about which more, presumably, anon), his body (the rest of it, which is to say, excluding the

2 He was the one, though, with the contacts; he was the establishment figure. I could never hope to compete with him on that score. Having said that, I was determined that what, by now, was seen as a meteoric rise in terms of my own career would not be thwarted by his superior nous and connections. I looked, in short, for holes in what he was saying and ways in which I could pin something on him to propel myself forwards at his expense, even though I knew this to be a profoundly risky thing to be doing.

legs, feet, and perhaps also the arms and hands) would, in fact, be at right angles to the ramp leading down towards, yet initially away from (as before) the pedestrian underpass proper and that this leaning would enable his left foot to complete the elegant arc in the form of the classical parabola that it had commenced at the moment it had left that sidewalk/pavement. In other words, his leaning progressively forwards from a position at right angles to the sidewalk to a position at right angles to the ramp would enable him to avoid the truncation of that parabola which might otherwise have occurred had he remained upright, which is to say, had his body, the rest thereof (as previously defined) remained at right angles to the sidewalk/pavement such that this would prevent his left foot from attaining the appropriate point beyond and below the landing point of his right foot – without, that is, a painful and unnatural stretch in that remainder of his body.

That this was in fact the case – that the remainder of his body had, roughly speaking, attained this right angle to the ramp at the moment that his left foot touched down, thereby enabling the centre-point of his left foot to complete the classical parabola that it had commenced tracing at the moment it had left the sidewalk or pavement upon which it had hitherto been placed – he noticed at the same time as noticing that, rather than following suit, as it were, the woman in the tight-fitting pinstriped suit had, in fact, stopped at the top of the steps leading down to the landing point of both ('his') slope and ('her') steps. And the reason she had stopped there, he thought, was so she could retrieve something from Richard Knox's briefcase, meaning not only that she could gain access to its locked interior but that Marguerite might, in time, do so too.

4

HAVING SAID THAT his body had attained an angle of ninety degrees, which is to say, a right angle, to the ramp at the moment that his left foot had touched down, in advance of his right foot, upon that ramp, he realised, as, feeling somewhat unbalanced (physically speaking), he reached out, with his right hand, for the handrail that was attached to the wall rising at right angles from the right side of the ramp and which descended, at a height suitable for gripping by the hand – left or right, depending on whether one was ascending or descending – of a typical adult subject (or, in the case of the handrail that ran in parallel to, but below, the aforementioned handrail, by the hand of a typical child, or adolescent, subject) and at an angle identical to that of the ramp itself (with a similar, although obverse, arrangement pertaining to the left (from his (and, presumably, for reasons ongoingly mysterious to him (if not to us), our) perspective)), that, in fact, his body, which is to say the main stem, to call it that, of the upper part thereof, must, in fact, have attained this right angle to the ramp *before* his left foot had touched down upon it, which is to say, *before* his left foot had touched down upon that ramp. And the reason he thought that this must, in fact, have been the case related to his assertion, whilst that foot – his left – was, as it were, in flight, that this progressive forward-leaning action by the remainder (or thereabouts) of his body would enable the centre-point of his left foot to complete the classical parabola that it had commenced tracing at the moment it had left the sidewalk or pavement upon which it had hitherto been placed. In other words, were he to have been correct in his assertion that, in the absence of this forward-leaning posture whose boundary conditions were a right angle to the sidewalk or pavement at commencement and a right angle to the ramp at completion, he would not have been able to trace fully, in all its classical geometrical simplicity, the parabola with his left foot that had commenced with the take-off, as it were, of that foot from the horizontal plane formed by the sidewalk/pavement that intersected the ramp leading down to the landing plane, to call it that, of ramp and stairs, then wouldn't he have had to attain that right angle to the ramp before his left foot had touched down upon it, which is to say, before his left foot had touched down upon that ramp, given that, in ordinary circumstances, which is to say, in circumstances wherein he would be as it were walking on the flat, there would be a slight leaning forwards in advance of the contact between the front foot and that flat ground?

He was not, of course, saying that he or any other human subject would, in walking (and leaving aside running, for now, as well as other forms of self-propulsion[3]) on the flat, move from a position of slightly leaning backwards (which, for our purposes, he defined, now, as moving from an angle of slightly less than ninety degrees) to slightly leaning forwards (which, again, for our – and his – purposes, he defined as moving to an angle of slightly more than ninety degrees, with both of these angles being measured, presumably with a protractor or

3   The first 'find' – that was what they called it – occurred some weeks later. They had people there ready to analyse what they unearthed as they went along, but they could hardly have been prepared for this: a human skull.

other similar instrument, to the sidewalk, pavement or other form of flat plane used as the test location). And the reason he was not saying this was not just because he had no-one, really, to say it to, the woman in the tight-fitting pinstriped suit being out of earshot, as it's known; no, the reason he was not saying it related to the fact that he thought it to be untrue, or rather that he thought it was only half-true; and in saying that he thought it to be only half-true he meant, in this case, that he took it to be precisely, or exactly, half-true in the sense that, in walking upon this flat test-plane we would only, he thought, adopt the forwards- and not the backwards-lean as we progressed in the manner described, which is to say, by walking in the usual manner. In other words, he took it to be true that, when walking on a flat plane, regardless of whether that flat plane consisted of a sidewalk or pavement (although the test plane must, he now realised, consist, for reasons that he may come on to, of solid ground, which ruled out the beach, for instance, as a potential location for this experiment) then one would lean slightly forwards as one neared the point of completion of the forwards step but one would *not* lean slightly backwards at the commencement of the next step, and he believed this to be, quite simply, for anatomical reasons, which is to say that it was for the simple reason that the majority of human subjects were, as it were, hinged in such a way that it was much easier to bend forwards, which is to say, to create an angle between the main parts of the lower and upper body such that one created an angle of slightly more than ninety degrees, based on the datum, or perhaps frame of reference, previously defined, than it was to bend backwards, which is to say, to create an angle between the main parts of the lower and upper body such that one created an angle of slightly less than ninety degrees based, of course, on the same datum or frame of reference (and leaving aside, for now, at least, the whole category of human subjects that one would define as 'unhinged').

This slight (or, in some subjects, more pronounced) forwards lean that took place towards the point of completion of a forwards step during the normal act of walking on a flat plane was, then, the reason, he now realised, his previous assertion, that his body had attained an angle of ninety degrees, which is to say, a right angle, to the ramp at the moment that his left foot had touched down, in advance of his right foot, upon that ramp was, in fact, incorrect and why his subsequent, revised, assertion that he must have attained that angle just prior to that foot touching down upon that surface, which is to say his left foot touching down upon the ramp that led (and, as far as we can tell, still leads) down to the horizontal rectangular plane that also formed the landing plane for the steps down which the woman in the tight-fitting pinstriped suit would, he hoped, eventually descend, was, he felt, correct.

5

HAVING SKETCHED THIS situation to his reasonable satisfaction, which is to say, having sketched this situation in a way that was reasonably satisfying to him rather than in a way that could be taken by others (including, perhaps, the lawyers) to be reasonably satisfying, he now found himself leaning back slightly (relative to his most recent position, rather than to the horizontal), as his right foot started to manoeuvre itself into a position whereby it could take flight, which is to say into a position from which to launch itself forwards hoping, to the extent that a bodily extremity of this type could hope, to find itself, before too long, in advance of the left foot once again, this being the nature of the perennial race between those two one-sided competitors, at least in the situation of the average able-bodied biped. And what he noticed, as he found himself roughly in a position in which his torso, at least, to call it that now, was more or less at a right-angle, once again, to the ramp leading down to the horizontal rectangular landing plane, given that he had leant backwards following the left foot's attainment of the solid surface of the ramp in advance of the right foot, was that this position, which is to say, this bodily arrangement, was not actually that comfortable – at least it would not have been that comfortable had it not been for the support provided by his outstretched right arm and hand, the latter being in contact with the right-handrail, which is to say the right-hand handrail. In other words, just because, on a flat, solid surface (with the requirement for solidity ruling out, as before, for those enthusiasts who were, or are, somehow following Marguerite's investigation from the beach, the definite article always, somehow, seeming appropriate in this regard even though, clearly, there is more than one, the use of that location to test these most recent hypotheses) one would typically walk with one's torso roughly at right-angles to that surface, a torso which would, as has been established to his reasonable satisfaction (as previously defined) lean slightly forwards with each step such that the angle that it would subtend with the horizontal might increase by, say, three degrees (not the band) each time, before reverting to the vertical, this did not mean that one would, or should, appropriate and approximate these angles regardless of the terrain that one would encounter outside of those test conditions. In still other words, what he was finding was that, even though he had established to his reasonable satisfaction (*op. cit.*) that were he as it were to be on the level, his torso and perhaps even his head would remain upright, this did not mean, now that he was steadily – rapidly, even – descending towards what he continued to refer to as the mouth of the pedestrian underpass proper, that his bodily disposition and orientation should, wholesale, follow suit, as it's known. Indeed, there must be a limit beyond which it could not go, given that, were the ramp angle to pass beyond a certain steepness, he would be prone to tumble, rather than to stride, as he continued to do in the current scenario, down it.

It was, then, the support provided by his right hand, arm and shoulder that was sustaining him at what he now took to be an unusual angle in the circumstances, as he continued to move down the ramp towards what he hoped would be his meeting point with the woman in the tight-fitting pinstriped suit, who, he noticed, had placed the ball of her right foot, in its high-heeled shoe, upon the dwarf wall that formed the base of the railings to the right of the steps leading down to the horizontal rectangular plane. More specifically it was the downward-sliding loose grip of his hand, the orientation of the arm (locked at the elbow such that the fore- and upper arm, to call them that, were in alignment and, unlike his torso, were maintaining an angle of ninety degrees to the *sidewalk* rather than the ramp) and the transmission of the support that this arrangement provided to the remainder of his body via its flexible connector, the shoulder, that had enabled him to move his torso from an angle of ninety degrees to the pavement to an angle of three degrees (as before) beyond ninety degrees to the ramp leading down towards the woman in the tight-fitting pinstriped suit and, he hoped, the successful culmination of his investigation into the disappearance of Harold Absalon, the Mayor's transport advisor, who had been missing for some time now, it would seem, to the extent that he was presumed, at least, to be dead.

6

HOW, HE NOW wondered, was he to proceed, given that, in terms of his progress down the ramp, he had completed one full cycle, which is to say that his right foot, having left the broad horizontal plane of the sidewalk/pavement, had crossed the threshold formed by that pavement with the ramp leading down to the less broad, but no less horizontal, rectangular plane that formed the landing- and the mid-point[4] of both the ramp leading down to the mouth of the pedestrian underpass proper and of the stairs leading down to same before landing upon that ramp, with his left foot having followed suit, as it's known, leaving him, or rather his respective feet, in a position from which to recommence the aforementioned cycle, albeit from an advanced position progressively speaking, although in absolute rather than relative terms, given the foregoing, which is to say in relation to his linear rather than cyclic starting point? And, in saying that this less broad, but no less horizontal, plane formed the landing- and the mid-point of both the ramp leading down to the mouth of the pedestrian underpass proper and of the stairs, he had immediately realised that neither of these was, in fact, the case, which is to say that that landing-point did not, in fact, form the mid-point of the ramp or of the stairs; and he wondered how he had made such an elementary error as this.

---

4 Then, one day, at a deeper level, albeit at a different site nearby: the complete skeletal remains of a woman head-to-toe with a child.

Could it be that he had meant to say that this landing-point (or, more precisely, plane) formed, at a sub-surface level, the mid-point – the intermediate plane – between surface- and underground-levels, rather than saying, as he had done, that it formed the mid-point of the ramp leading down to the mouth of the pedestrian underpass proper as well as of the stairs? Granted that he may have been thinking of the ramps that connected with this mid-point but which led in opposite directions – the one in front of him down towards the plane itself and the other down towards the mouth of the subway/ pedestrian underpass proper (or, for those emerging from that underpass and wishing to ascend to the surface, the one *up* towards the plane itself and the other *up* towards the sidewalk/ pavement) – as one ramp, which is to say as a ramp that, as it were, folded back upon itself, but which, around its mid-point, flattened out and progressed, momentarily, in a traverse, rather than in a back and forth (or forth and back) direction before continuing as a downward (or, depending, upward) incline. If, in other words, one took this whole sweep of flat plane, whether inclined or otherwise, as being 'the ramp', then it would seem reasonable to assert, as Marguerite had done at the outset of this branch of his inquiry, that, either side of its mid-point it levelled out, momentarily, in the way so inadequately described, such that this levelling out formed the mid-point of the ramp down which Marguerite continued to move in pursuit of his investigative objectives. Where it fell down, though, as it were, was as soon as one tried to apply the same logic to the aforementioned stairs, and this was where he had realised that, to continue the metaphor, he had stumbled in his ordinarily impeccable logic. In other words, were one to apply, by extension (presumably), the same reasoning to

the stairs in front of the woman in the tight-fitting pinstriped
suit then one could see that the logic crumbled (to change
the metaphor, although it could be that this crumbling of the
logic had, in fact, caused the aforementioned stumble and
fall). In no way, in short, could the intermediate plane be
said to be at the mid-point of the stairs given that the stairs
decisively terminated at the point where they met that landing
point (hence the name that he had adopted for it hitherto, he
thought, although equally it could of course be taken to be
a *launching* point – or, more properly, landing- and launch-
ing-*plane* – depending on one's perspective). It could not, in
other words, be asserted that the stairs continued past the
point of that landing; those wishing to continue to descend
to underground-, subway- or underpass-level would need to
do so via the ramp leading down to the mouth (as before)
of the pedestrian underpass proper, a ramp, remember, that
he could (or we can, or both) take either as part of the ramp
that commenced its journey, with Marguerite in the current
case, at surface-, sidewalk- or pavement-level, continuing its
descent at a sub-surface level via the horizontal landing (or
launching) plane previously alluded to, or as commencing at
the point where it met that landing (etc.) point, which is to
say at the mid-point between surface- (etc.) and underground-
(etc.) level. It was for this reason, then, that he sought now
to correct his records in the manner described, which is to
say, why he sought to clarify that, rather than being at the
mid-point of the ramp or stairs leading down to the mouth
of the subway, it was much more accurate to assert that this
horizontal rectangular plane, to the extent that it was in an
intermediate position, was intermediate between surface- (etc.)
and underground- (etc.) level, and, further, why, throughout

(he thought), he preferred to refer to the ramp leading down *to* that intermediate level as being a separate entity to the ramp that led *from* it down to the mouth of the pedestrian underpass proper. He would endeavour to use these naming conventions throughout the remainder of his investigation, to the extent that he remembered to do so.

7

I T MAY BE as simple as that, he thought, as his right heel
raised itself from the ground, which is to say that it raised
itself from the ramp as a precursor to that whole foot pro-
jecting itself further down the ramp towards the intermediate
plane that the last chapter[5] was at such pains to explore (if,
indeed, a chapter can be at pains, or can explore, or both –
not that Marguerite could have any conception of what a
chapter was, or is, in the context of his ongoing investigation into the disappearance of Harold Absalon, the Mayor's
transport advisor, who was missing presumed dead), even
though, in doing so, which is to say, even though, in raising
itself from the inclined plane leading down to that intermediate point, it had gone against the main mission sub-objective,
which was to descend the ramp. In other words: Marguerite's
mission sub-objective was to descend the inclined plane
initially leading away from the sidewalk/pavement and
towards a horizontal rectangular plane that was, as before (and
ongoingly, one presumes), at an intermediate, sub-surface level.
Why, he now wondered, did he take this step, as it were, of
raising the heel of his right foot, which is to say the heel of
his battered right boot (were he to be wearing boots and,

5   The project view was it was too early, at that stage, to say from which
    period these and the other unearthed items belonged – shards of household
    objects, wax wooden tablets with written indentations, copper alloy coins.
    This did not stop Knox from appearing on our screens almost immediately
    to account for them.

if he were, were they to be battered in the sense of being worn) given that this action on his part seemingly went against what he was trying to achieve in this part of his mission, which is to say that it went against his mission sub-objective of descending the first ramp and traversing the horizontal rectangular plane, thereby making contact, he hoped, en route to the pedestrian underpass proper, with the woman in the tight-fitting pinstriped suit who, he noticed, had also raised the heel of her right foot, in its high-heeled shoe, whose ball was placed upon the dwarf wall that formed the base of the railings to the right of the steps leading down to that horizontal rectangular plane? Would it not have been better to ensure that every part of his body, every fulcrum and data point, continued in a downwards trajectory; surely this would have been the most conducive strategy to achieving his sub-objective of attaining that intermediate, sub-surface level and making the aforementioned contact?

As he raised his heel further he realised that, in fact, this heel had, as it were, started its ascent long before his left foot had touched down in advance of his right, which is to say that, given the foregoing assertion that his body remained at roughly right angles to the line of the slope, aside, of course, from the moment, or thereabouts, when his left foot had made contact with that slope, rather than remaining roughly at right angles to the pavement/sidewalk from which he had commenced this descent, that his heel-ascension, if one can call it that without evoking overtly religious imagery, must have occurred so as to facilitate the upper body orientation that he had previously referred to, and not just because the lower half, or thereabouts, of his body was not limber enough to remain in straightened circumstances whilst the upper half (as before) adopted the previously referred-to orientation. He needed, in short, to raise that heel, just as, no doubt, when he next took a step with his left foot, having rapidly, he hoped, completed the step with his right that he had just commenced, he would have to raise the heel of that foot, and not just at the moment when he was ready to complete that step but, as in the current situation, well in advance of its completion so as to retain his forward leaning (and thinking) in relation (the leaning) to the plane of the sidewalk/pavement from whence he had commenced this branch of his investigation into the disappearance of Harold Absalon, the Mayor's transport advisor, who remained missing presumed dead.

In retaining, then, the angle of ninety degrees to the ramp, in the same way as he had retained that angle to the sidewalk/pavement prior to commencing his descent (leaving aside, momentarily, the previously reported circumstances in which this angle was momentarily exceeded), he would need, he realised, to raise both heels (not necessarily simultaneously), even though this, seemingly, went against the general trend of descent that he was trying so diligently to cultivate; and the reason he would need to go as it were against the stream in this way was, he thought, to do with maintaining the aforementioned angle of the upper half, roughly speaking, of his body (again with the caveat of the momentary exceedance of same), given the advantages that that orientation brought to his investigation into the disappearance of the missing transport advisor. It would, he thought, in short, be much more difficult to retain this angle were he not repeatedly to raise his heels in turn, and long before touchdown of the opposite foot.

Indeed it may even be that at the moment the airborne foot passes the emplanted (if not implanted) foot, the heel of the latter starts, each time, its ascent, such that the airborne foot, having reached the zenith of the parabola that it was tracing through a longitudinal section at right angles to the plane of the ramp, starts its descent at the very moment the opposite heel starts its ascent as a precursor to the commencement of the ascent of the remainder of that foot, an ascent that could only really be said to properly commence, he thought, at the moment the ball of that foot took off, as it were, from the surface of that ramp at the very start of tracing the parabola that the preceding foot will just have completed, with this newly initiated parabola, whilst starting at a location behind the landing point of the previous parabola, terminating at a position in advance of it (otherwise what was the point of it all?). And it was, perhaps, a law of motion that he had discovered through this inquiry, one in which the relationship between the feet of one descending a ramp is such as to conserve ascension. And he gave this law of motion the perhaps predicable title 'The Conservation of Ascension Law (relating to the feet of someone descending a ramp)' whilst realising, as he noticed that the woman in the tight-fitting pinstriped suit had placed Richard Knox's briefcase upon her right thigh, which had been raised at an angle of approximately forty-five degrees to the horizontal by the aforementioned placement of the ball of her right foot, in its high-heeled shoe, upon the dwarf wall, and the raising of that heel to that purpose, that it needed to be further tested in the field and in the lab.

He had realised, in the course of this inquiry, that it wasn't just his heel(s) that seemed, momentarily, to go against the sub-objective of descent that he had set himself in this part of his investigation: the airborne foot was also, during its phase of ascent, clearly (given the description of this phase) going against the general presumption towards descent. How, he now wondered, as the heel of his right foot, having reached the full extent of its ascension whilst the ball of the same foot remained in contact with the ramp, precipitated that foot's take-off from the slope it had hitherto been connected to via what's known as its ball, given this and the law of conservation of ascension that he had coined and been rightly recognised for, could he be descending towards the pedestrian underpass at all?

8

THERE IS, THEN, a situation in which the right foot, having now taken off, as it's known, was going against the general presumption in favour of descent, he thought, as he noticed that the woman in the tight-fitting pinstriped suit was holding the left side of the briefcase with her left hand as she reached, with her right, for what he presumed to be the combination lock located to the right of the right-hand clasp. The thing that reassured Marguerite was the fact that his foot, at least, was moving forwards. Yet even here, it could be said, as he heard for the first time the sound of wheels on the sidewalk behind him, small wheels, these, travelling from the right, wheels attached to an as-yet unidentified carrier, that his foot was going against a further mission sub-objective of travelling towards and through the mouth, as he's taken to calling it, of the pedestrian underpass proper. In other words, just as the mouth of the pedestrian underpass proper was at an elevation such that moving towards it involved a descent (whereas his right foot continued to *a*scend), so with his horizontal direction – he was, in fact, on his current trajectory, momentarily moving *away* from the mouth of the pedestrian underpass proper. How had he found himself at this juncture? What had led an investigator of his calibre to such foolishness?

It related, he thought, to the fact of the human anatomy and the need to keep it intact – in short, the need to make the transition gradually, rather than all at once. Otherwise one might injure oneself, and one was always, in his experience, keen to avoid that. It is a trade-off, then, between intactness, to call it that, and directness – that seemed to be the situation he was involved in at that moment, in the sense that, with his right foot moving up (up) and away from the mouth of the pedestrian underpass to which he hoped, ultimately (within the current mission sub-objective) to head, via the intermediate, sub-surface level so as to make contact with the woman in the tight-fitting pinstriped suit, it would seem that he was literally taking one step back from that goal. However, were he to have attempted to move directly to that location, which is to say to the mouth of the pedestrian underpass proper, from surface-, which is to say pavement- or sidewalk-, level then it was quite likely that he would have done a more or less serious injury to himself to the extent that he might not have been able to continue to proceed through that underpass in the fashion that he wished to proceed, which is to say by putting one foot in front of the other (or thereabouts[6]). So what it would make up for in terms of directness it would have more than lost in relation to bodily intactness, must have been his judgement as he'd passed directly above that point, which is to say above the mouth of the pedestrian underpass proper, en route to the ramp that he continued to descend towards that location, despite the fact that the trajectory of his airborne right foot appeared to go against this, in that it was currently moving upwards, and away from, the entrance, to call it that, of the pedestrian underpass proper.

Yet there were some who would more or less happily have

6 The experts thought these were plague victims, he said, who had suffered and died hundreds of years previously. I knew the truth to be quite different, but at that stage could prove nothing.

made that more direct, more abrupt, transition from surface to underground level by vaulting, might be the term, the railings located directly above the mouth of the subway, railings designed, and constructed, to prevent those walking close to the area in which they had been installed from inadvertently making that abrupt transition, which is to say from inadvertently falling from sidewalk- to subway-level. These railings, which would be of a height that was at least half as high as the average human subject, he thought, and which were designed and constructed to act as a deterrent to making abrupt transitions in height – particularly where those transitions involved moving from a higher to a lower location – would, then, have to be vaulted, hurdled or jumped, would, he thought, be the main options, such that, despite the deterrence in the form of the railings, typically, that, as before, he thought, would have to be at least half as high as the average human subject (this for subsidiary and not unrelated safety reasons), one would determinedly make that transition, having, notice, momentarily, to go against one's mission sub-objective of abrupt descent by an abrupt *ascent*, in the form of that vault, hurdle, jump or, granted (in exceptional cases), hop over the guard rail, as it would perhaps be called, which is to say the rail that had been installed there to guard against the abrupt transitions in height that would otherwise perhaps more routinely occur, by forcing one to make an abrupt transition in height in the opposite direction to the one in which one wished to move, which is to say that it forced one abruptly (or, for the climbers, somewhat less abruptly) upwards so that one could be in a position, with gravity on one's side this time, to make the abrupt downwards transition that would take one more directly to the mouth of the pedestrian underpass proper – more directly, at least, than the route that Marguerite, in the form of his right foot, seemed to be taking as he continued his descent to what he more poetically thought of, once again, as the bowels, or the underworld, of that once-great city.

He was reassured, then, that, on reflection, he was not *so* different, after all, to those criminals (or errant investigators, such as his so-called investigative colleague who had been on his trail previously[7]) who opted to make the more abrupt transition from surface to sub-surface level in moving more directly than he to the entrance of the pedestrian underpass proper. Both he, and they, would need to go against their shared mission sub-objective of descent in that, in his scenario, his feet (and, at the current moment, whatever that means, specifically his right foot) must *a*scend somewhat, in turn, before they could *de*scend (and he wondered, somehow, whether using *a*scend and *de*scend might have been better in terms of italicisation given the remaining portion that these words shared) just as, in theirs, their whole body must ascend, by whatever means (including, of course, the pogo) such that they, and it, are/is propelled, in their and its entirety, above what Marguerite has taken to referring to as the guard rail before, of course, their, and its, more precipitous descent.

Perhaps, then, the only difference between him and them was that, as well as having to partially (in his case, which is to say in the form of his right foot, currently) and wholly (in their situation) ascend, he, in addition, must move horizontally away from the underground entrance to the pedestrian subway before turning, via the intermediate, sub-surface level, to face

7 I couldn't show my face on site, of course, but would receive reports of the painstaking work of unearthing and interpretation that went on daily. I asked Hazel to keep me abreast of developments, and took to conducting my own late-night researches in the labyrinthine archives under City Hall.

it, as it were, whereas, in terms of horizontal direction, the leapers, vaulters, hoppers, jumpers and/or pogoers need not, even for a moment (given their directness), go horizontally against their sub-objective of moving towards the entrance to the subway.

Yet once again, on reflection, he realised, as his right foot continued its ascent, that those agents and provocateurs who took the more direct approach that he had adumbrated would, in fact, at least marginally, have to go against their sub-objective of moving towards that entrance in that their momentum, generated through the inevitable run-up, would take them marginally away from that entrance (this in the case where they cleared the guard rail, which is to say without contact); in the case where they used the guard rail, steeplechase-style, to secure the necessary height to clear it then, still, this, Marguerite thought, would result in a momentum that would take them, albeit ever-so-slightly, horizontally away from the below-ground entrance to the pedestrian underpass proper.

Their situations were, then, in conclusion, not dissimilar, he thought, in that one needed, in both instances, to move both horizontally and vertically – wholly or partially – in the direction that was the opposite of one's desires (although he was, he noted, still moving towards the woman in the tight-fitting pinstriped suit, whom he certainly desired, and who, at that moment, was leaning slightly forwards and to the right towards the briefcase that was placed upon her right thigh, which had been raised at an angle of approximately forty-five degrees to the horizontal by the aforementioned placement of the ball of her right foot, in its high-heeled shoe, upon the dwarf wall, and the raising of that heel to that purpose, to scrutinise, Marguerite thought, the rotary numerals of the combination lock to the right of the briefcase's right-hand clasp), albeit more abruptly in the case of those who travelled, more directly, in the manner that he had not inadequately, he thought, described. The only differences, then, seemed to be temporal and physical: one took the physical risk, in the case of the abrupt transition, so as to gain a temporal advantage on one's pursuers (or on those one was pursuing). It was a risk that, clearly, he'd been unwilling – or unable – to countenance.

9

HIS INSTINCT, HAVING heard the sound of wheels travelling along the sidewalk behind and to the right of him was that he was, now, being pursued, that his pursuer would attempt to make contact with the woman in the tight-fitting pinstriped suit before he did, and that he must, at all costs, prevent this from occurring. He needed, then, rapidly to plot the course of the next stage of his investigation, as his right foot continued its ascent in furtherance of his general presumption in favour of descent towards the woman in the tight-fitting pinstriped suit; yet, at the same time, in the absence of further information as to the nature of those wheels, he felt he had insufficient evidence with which to do so – all he had to go on, as it's known, was the assertion, made earlier in this narrative (not that he had a sense of a narrative or of narrative time – just, presumably, his own time, as it were, elapsing on the ground, so to speak), that the wheels in question were small, which could, of course, encompass much in terms of category of wheel, with the largest in this range perhaps being exemplified by that used on a wheelbarrow, and the smallest being exemplified by those used on the equally eponymous wheeled suitcase. In between these two extremes lay, he thought, any number of small-wheeled non-motorised vehicles used to propel the human subject and its cargo (plus the resulting detritus). In other words, between the two dimensional (not two-dimensional) extremes, as he envisaged them (usefully making that vision available to us through means that must, of necessity, remain elusive if not downright unfathomable to him) of the wheelbarrow and the wheeled suitcase lay a whole family of small-wheeled non-motorised vehicles, a family whose members included skateboards, roller-blades and -skates (but not, of course, ice-skates), the non-motorised scooter, the pushchair, the transport wheelchair (which is to say, the wheelchair designed not to be propelled any distance by its occupant), the parcel trolley, the hand cart, the trolley-bag, the pram, the stroller, meals on wheels and the wheelie bin. Indeed these latter examples introduced an important distinction that he needed most urgently to turn his attention to on the ground, as it were – in relation, that is, to the small-wheeled non-motorised vehicle that he took to be approaching the ramp leading down to the horizontal rectangular plane from behind and to the right of him: the distinction between those small-wheeled non-motorised vehicles that were used to propel oneself and those used to propel someone or something else, such as goods, garden waste, garbage, parcels, luggage, an old person or a child, to give only the primary examples. And the reason he needed, most urgently, to turn his attention to this distinction in relation to the small-wheeled non-motorised vehicle that was approaching the ramp leading down to the horizontal rectangular plane from behind and to the right of him was, quite simply, the following: were his pursuer to be propelling themselves, then this made it more likely in Marguerite's estimation that they would not only gain on him, as it's known, and overtake him, but they would also, he thought, intercept the woman in the tight-fitting pinstriped suit before he himself had done so, thereby jeopardising his investigation into the disappearance of Harold Absalon, the

Mayor's transport advisor, who was missing presumed dead, and increasing the likelihood that Marguerite would befall the exact same fate; whereas were they to be propelling something or someone else, such as goods, garden waste, garbage, parcels, luggage, an old person or a child, then, simply put, this reduced the likelihood of the aforementioned eventualities occurring given that, in this latter scenario, the person doing the propelling would most likely be travelling more slowly given the cumbersomeness of those goods, persons etc. that they were propelling, meaning, in short, that they would take longer to overtake him making it less likely that they would intercept the woman in the tight-fitting pinstriped suit before he himself had done so.

That it was the latter scenario that was, in fact, unfolding, which is to say that the wheels in question belonged to a parcel trolley, wheeled suitcase or the like, rather than being used as a means of self-propulsion, as it were, was borne out, Marguerite thought, by the sound of footsteps emanating from the vicinity of, and, Marguerite thought, accompanying, those small wheels behind and to the right of him, and it was this conclusion that led him, fatally, momentarily, to relax.

10

WHILST THE PERSON propelling the parcel trolley, wheeled suitcase or the like would, given the cumbersomeness of their cargo, be travelling more slowly than someone propelling themselves on a small-wheeled non-motorised vehicle, they might, Marguerite thought, compensate for this relative lack of speed with an increased manoeuvrability; what he meant to say by this was that, whilst the person propelling the small-wheeled non-motorised vehicle behind and to the right of him might take more time to gain on him, as it's known, than in the scenario in which they were propelling themselves in the manner described (that is, using a skateboard, rollerblades or the like), it would, he thought, be easier for them, once they had done so, which is to say, once they had eventually gained on him, to manoeuvre that non-motorised vehicle around him. The reason for this was that, in that case, which is to say, in the case where the person was propelling a parcel trolley, wheeled suitcase or the like rather than propelling themselves on a small-wheeled non-motorised vehicle such as a skateboard or rollerblades, the feet of the person propelling that trolley or suitcase would be in contact with the ramp down which it, they (the propellant) and Marguerite (who, remember, continued to investigate the disappearance of Harold Absalon, the Mayor's transport advisor, who was missing presumed dead) were moving, thereby providing an enhanced manoeuvrability, for reasons he would, he hoped, come on to. The feet of that person would not, of course, be continually in touch with that surface; were that to be the case then it is difficult to imagine how that person could propel, let alone manoeuvre, themselves or their non-motorised vehicle down the slope in question. No, in the case of the biped (and we needn't limit ourselves, in this instance, to the more evolved in that category), it would, Marguerite thought, be the case that one or more (to an upper limit of two) of those feet would be in contact with the surface at any one time. This was in the situation, of course, where the bipedic subject (to call them that) was not running, since, when one is running, one or *less* (which is to say, one or none, or, rather, one or neither) of one's feet is in fact, in contact with the surface that one is running upon. Could he be certain that the person behind and to the right of him was not, in fact running, he wondered? He could not be certain; yet the fact was that he heard no running, which is to say that the only sound he could hear was that of walking – aside, that is, from the sound that the small wheels of the small-wheeled non-motorised vehicle made as they trundled, if that was what they were doing, across the paving stones behind and to the right of him as they approached the ramp leading down to the horizontal rectangular plane that also formed the landing plane for the steps down which the woman in the tight-fitting pinstriped suit would, he hoped, eventually descend.

Why, then, he wondered, had the rhythmic interval of the sound made by the wheels themselves now abruptly doubled, whilst the rhythm and speed of the footsteps remained constant and were indicative of steady-state walking, suggesting that the non-motorised vehicle itself was now, in fact, travelling at twice the speed it had hitherto been travelling at? It was to this conundrum with all its implications, no doubt, for the city authorities, the nation state – and maybe even the planet that we are all, presumably, inhabiting – that he must now, urgently, turn his not insubstantial investigative nous towards.

11

THE SOUND OF the wheels and of the footsteps on the paving stones of the sidewalk or pavement might yield something further, might it not? What did he have in mind here, he wondered, as he noticed that the left hand of the woman in the tight-fitting pinstriped suit had joined her right in manipulating, he thought, the rotary numerals of the combination lock to the right of the right-hand clasp of the briefcase that was placed upon her right thigh, which had been raised at an angle of approximately forty-five degrees to the horizontal by the aforementioned placement of the ball of her right foot, in its high-heeled shoe, upon the dwarf wall, and the raising of that heel to that purpose? What he had in mind, he thought, was that the sound of those small wheels and of the footsteps that Marguerite had taken to be associated with them might, if one listened intently enough to them, yield something further of the nature of: those wheels and footsteps themselves; what they were in contact with; and, by extension (a bit of a leap this), any intentions that those responsible for those sounds had with regard to Marguerite and to the woman in the tight-fitting pinstriped suit, who, Marguerite believed, wished to assist him, which is to say, wished to assist Marguerite in his investigation into the disappearance of Harold Absalon, the Mayor's transport advisor, who was missing presumed dead. He felt, now, as his right foot approached a zenith in this portion of its forward motion towards the horizontal rectangular plane that was the landing position not only of the ramp down which he continued to move in this way but also of the flight of steps down which the woman in the tight-fitting pinstriped suit would, he hoped, imminently descend, that he must take each of these propositions in turn and explore further what he meant by them so as to expose, to his auditors (which is to say, to us, following his peregrinations and prognostications via means that were, of necessity, ongoingly mysterious, if not downright unfathomable, to him), how he had arrived, in his mind, at the conclusion that, were he to attend intently to those sounds, that this would yield something further that could, crucially, provide not only an indication of what the sounds' source's (or, indeed, sounds' sources') intentions were towards him and to the woman in the tight-fitting pinstriped suit but also the breakthrough that Marguerite sought in his investigation into the disappearance of Harold Absalon, the Mayor's transport advisor who, remember, was missing presumed dead.

Firstly, then, the premise that the sound of the wheels and of the footsteps that Marguerite had taken to be associated with them would yield something further of the nature of both. All he had in mind here was that, were the sounds indicative of hard wheels and/or heels, then this might exclude certain types or even styles of self-propelled small-wheeled non-motorised vehicle – the wheelbarrow, the wheelchair and most commercial forms of parcel trolley, for instance – as well as perhaps being suggestive of someone who was what's known as 'well-heeled', someone, that is, like the woman in the tight-fitting pinstriped suit in her elegant footwear, or Isobel Absalon, the wife of the missing transport advisor, who had previously been on Marguerite's trail[8], which might, in turn, further suggest that the self-propelled small-wheeled non-motorised vehicle was what's known as a 'carry-on', which is to say a two-wheeled suitcase beloved, in particular, of the business classes because it was suitable for stowage as cabin luggage in an aircraft, thus avoiding a potentially lengthy wait at the baggage carousel or even a prohibitive additional charge in the circumstance where one exceeded what's known as one's baggage allowance.

Pleased with the not insignificant progress seemingly afforded by just this first premise he moved decisively on to the second: that were one to attend (which is to say, to listen) intently enough to the sounds of those wheels and of the footsteps that Marguerite had taken to be associated with them then this would yield data and/or information about what those wheels and feet were in contact with, particularly given the rhythmic nature of those sounds, the rhythm in the first instance being in part dependent on the distance between the interstices that were the interface between the paving stones of the sidewalk/pavement such that, were the size or shape of those paving stones to change, or were the surfacing material to change altogether – from, say, paving stones to flagstones, flagstones to brick weave, brick weave to cobbles, or cobbles to blisters (to name just some of the myriad of possibilities) – then the rhythmic interval, which is to say the frequency, of the sound that the semi-rigid wheels of that self-propelled small-wheeled non-motorised vehicle made as it moved over that surface would change accordingly, with

8 Each time I intuited that I might be onto something – certain patterns re-emerging or familiar individuals re-surfacing – I found a crucial piece of evidence – the transcript of an interview, an artefact, a microfiche sheet – either to have been partially redacted or to be absent entirely.

this change, in the situation where the constituent elements of the surfacing in question – the pavement or sidewalk in this instance – transitioned abruptly from, say, paving stones that were twice as large as the subsequent flagstones, being equivalent (all else being equal) to a doubling in frequency suggestive to those monitoring this situation aurally but not visually (which was, of course, Marguerite's situation as well as ours, by extension) of a doubling of vehicular speed, which is to say a doubling of the speed of that non-motorised vehicle (leaving aside, for now if not in perpetuity, the more complex interaction between a *four-* as opposed to a two-wheeled self-propelled small-wheeled non-motorised vehicle, such as the supermarket trolley, the four-wheeled suitcase or the baggage trolley, particularly one whose wheel-spacing did not correspond precisely to the width or length of the constituents of the surface in question) which, roughly speaking, was what Marguerite had perceived in the moments leading up to the onset of this urgent, comprehensive though not yet exhaustive study, which is to say, a doubling of the rhythmic frequency, regardless of whether this corresponded, in fact, to a doubling in speed or to a halving of interstitial distance. Given that the sounds of the footsteps would remain unaffected by the size of the paving material used in that sidewalk or pavement, the anomaly between the rhythmic frequency of the wheels and the footsteps could, then, be accounted for, quite simply, by a reduction in the size of those constituent elements at the crucial moment.

What this did not (and could not) account for, Marguerite thought, as he noticed that the footsteps had now moved to a position that was behind him to his left, was the in-creasing dissociation between the sounds of the wheels and those of the footsteps such that the latter, while remaining at the same frequency, which is to say, whilst remaining at a rhythmic frequency indicative of steady-state walking, were progressively decreasing in amplitude, which is to say that they were getting quieter, indicating that the feet in question were moving away from him, to the left, at the level of the sidewalk or pavement, whilst the former – the sound of the wheels of the small-wheeled non-motorised vehicle, which, he judged, were now emanating from a position more directly behind him and to his left – had increased both in frequency and in amplitude, suggesting that they were, in fact, rolling, or being rolled, down the ramp towards him, and were, he now belatedly realised to his embarrassment and surprise, nothing to do with the footsteps, and had never been anything to do with them, so far as he could tell.

Given that the slabs, to call them that, of the ramp leading down towards the horizontal rectangular plane were not, in fact, progressively decreasing in size compared to those of the sidewalk/pavement, the fact that the wheels' rhythmic frequency had abruptly doubled (and continued to increase), would, he thought, indicate that the wheels, which he now thought were being used by someone to propel themselves, rather than goods, refuse, luggage or another person of whatever age, were, quite simply, speeding up, as he lengthened his pace, mid-stride, in response to them; this he took as an all-too-immediate example of his third premise: that the person propelling themselves in this way was intent upon getting to the woman in the tight-fitting pinstriped suit before Marguerite himself had done so and that, were they to succeed, this would not only jeopardise Marguerite's investigation into the disappearance of Harold Absalon, the Mayor's transport advisor, who was missing presumed dead, it would also increase significantly the likelihood that Marguerite himself would befall the exact same fate.

12

A T THIS STAGE Marguerite made a decision that he
knew would have profound consequences for his investigation: he chose to let go of the right-hand handrail – this
so that he could stray – or swerve – further over to the left,
the length of his right arm having constrained, until now, the
scope for this type of manoeuvre. And what he had in mind
here was that, were he to occupy more of the area to the left
of the ramp, which is to say the area on the left side of the
ramp rather than the area *to* the left of the ramp (which was,
of course, at the level of the pavement or sidewalk rather than
at the descending depth of the ramp itself) then this might
impede the progress of the self-propeller of (which is to say
the person who propelled themselves on) the still unidentified small-wheeled non-motorised vehicle. In other words
(and this would be another way of expressing it, which, in
itself, is another way of expressing 'in other words'), were he
to occupy the area, to the left, of the ramp (only the addition
of the punctuation providing the variant on this occasion)
then this would, he thought, serve to impede the now rapidly
descending but still unidentified rider-propelled small-wheeled
non-motorised vehicle which, in turn, might enable Marguerite
to attain the waypoint that was the woman in the tight-fitting
pinstriped suit in advance, still, of this rider-propelled small-
wheeled non-motorised vehicle, thereby continuing to support
his investigative efforts, as it were, which is to say his efforts

to unearth the circumstances surrounding the disappearance of Harold Absalon, the Mayor's transport advisor, who was missing presumed dead.

Clearly he would be doing this mid-stride (or thereabouts); in other words, he would, when he did (and it would seem that he hadn't done so yet), which is to say when he officially (as it were) let go of the right-hand handrail (and note that he had started to loosen his grip on this handrail, which is to say that he had started to loosen the grip that his right hand had on this right-hand handrail) then he would be doing this mid-stride (or thereabouts), given the imperative, for him, of taking decisive, swift action in this regard due to his relatively slow response, by his own standards, to the sounds of that small-wheeled non-motorised vehicle and the increasing speed with which he took his nemesis (as he now assumed the -boarder or scooter, to call the latter that, for now, to be) to be moving. In other words, given that he was mid-stride, or thereabouts (in fact, he noticed that he was marginally, still, in advance of mid-stride, which is to say that the foot in question was still to attain the zenith of the arc that it was tracing, through the air, but that it would imminently do so), and that he must decisively and swiftly change his own course so as to bring about a decisive, swift change in the course of his investigation (so as, presumably, to bring that investigation to a swift, decisive resolution), then he could not wait until that airborne foot had, for example, attained *terra firma* once again before acting to implement the aforementioned change of physical (and investigative) course, an action whose implementation, remember, would commence, he believed, at the moment when he released his right hand (which continued its as it were preparatory loosening) from the right-hand handrail.

Was it the difficulty, then, of the manoeuvre that he needed, swiftly and decisively, to engage in that was giving him pause in terms of swiftly and decisively engaging in it by letting go of, rather than progressively just loosening his grip on, the handrail that, as it were, ran down the right-hand side of the ramp-well (to call it that, utilising and amending the obvious analogical equivalent – the stairwell – even though, in the case of the ramp it was necessarily a much more elongated area thereby, in fact, undermining its resemblance to the as it were *ur*-well, the water-well)? In a sense he thought it was; yet the difficulty he had in mind would, he thought, resolve itself satisfactorily within the next few moments (or thereabouts) and then, he was sure, he would swiftly and decisively move to implement the change of course in his descent into the bowels, to call them that again, of the city, thereby impeding, and slowing, the descent of his wheeled pursuer which, in turn, he thought, would change the course of his investigation and of his pursuer's attempts at thwarting that investigation. And the difficulty he had in mind was simply that it was his right foot (he'd noticed, having perhaps referred back to previous chapters) that was approaching, and had now attained, the mid-point of its lengthened stride (which is to say at the precise instant of the apprehension by us of that word 'now', even though, strangely, the moment of apprehension of that word 'now' would vary, perhaps enormously, from person to person), which meant that it would have to negotiate, in moving swiftly and decisively to the left so that he could use his body to impede the progress of his wheeled pursuer down the left side of that ramp, his left leg, in a way that, had his left leg been mid-stride, or thereabouts, it would not have had to have done. In other words, were it to have been his

48

left leg that was mid-stride at the moment that Marguerite decided that he had to act decisively and swiftly to change his course so as to change *the* course (etc., as before) then, upon deciding this, he could immediately have moved, as it were, to implement the transposition of that foot to its new co-ordinates on the leftmost half (when viewing it lengthways) of that initial downwards (etc.) ramp leading to the horizontal rectangular plane that it shared, as it were, with the stair*way* (and not -well, in this instance) down which the woman in the tight-fitting pinstriped suit would, he hoped, imminently descend, since there would have been no other leg in the way of his left leg, which is to say, more specifically, that there would have been no other of *his* legs in the way of his left leg in its movement to a new co-ordinate position to his left and in front of him[9], lower down the slope, whereas, for his right leg, in this manoeuvre to the left, in advance and lower than its current location, it would have to pass the left leg, and it was for this reason that he had waited until now (as before), which is to say until the moment that it had just passed the mid-point (i.e. the zenith of the elongated arc that it was tracing through the air) of its trajectory, to decisively and swiftly change its course (etc.) by releasing, now (*ibid.*), the grip that his right hand had hitherto had on the right-hand handrail and pointing that right foot to the left, which is to say, rotating it counter-clockwise in mid-air (or thereabouts) towards its newly projected landing position, safe, finally, in the knowledge that his left leg would not, now, impede the latter's progress in the way that it would have done even

9 I arrived in the project office earlier than usual one morning, on the brink of despairing completely after another fruitless night of archival research. I was astonished to find that my office had been reassigned: my name removed from the door, my personal effects entirely replaced by another's.

moments earlier, with momentous consequences not just for his investigation into the disappearance of Harold Absalon, the Mayor's transport advisor, who was, remember, missing presumed dead, but for Marguerite himself – and, somehow, by extension, for each one of us.

13

HIS RIGHT FOOT was, or is, now pointing towards its projected landing position. Note, however, that it was, or is, not pointing directly at that position, in the same way that an aircraft, having taken off, or even whilst in mid-, or higher, air, does not point directly at its destination, but, instead, stays, Marguerite thought, more or less level, just as his foot, in moving towards its destination, would, he thought stay fairly level. What he was trying to say here, as he noticed that the woman in the tight-fitting pinstriped suit was no longer leaning slightly forwards and to the right, indicating, he thought, that she had only now entered the correct combination and opened, with her right hand, the briefcase's right-hand clasp, was that it was only in plan view, which is to say, when looking from above, that his right foot, having attained the zenith of the arc of the particular specific step that it was in the process of executing, was now pointing towards it purported, altered landing position. It could not, in other words, be said to be pointing at that landing position when viewed from the side, from the point of view of the woman in the tight-fitting pinstriped suit, say; nor, he thought, could his wheeled pursuer, viewing him, presumably like us, from the rear, given that they (his wheeled pursuer), and we (who are pursuing him via other means ongoingly mysterious to him) are, as it were, following in his footsteps, correctly assert that Marguerite's right foot was pointing at its new landing position; in both (and other) cases it would be correct, Marguerite thought, to assert that the foot was, in fact, pointing to a co-ordinate within the lower section of the far wall, a wall that formed the left-hand boundary of the ramp downwards to what he had started calling the mutual landing point for that ramp and the steps leading down to it or up from it; or, for those who were ascending the ramp from that landing point (which remained, note, an empty category), the *right*-hand boundary of the ramp *upwards from* that landing point. Yet he could assert, rightly, he thought, that, in plan view, his right foot was pointing in the direction of its revised purported landing position; at least it was, in this view, pointing to a (perhaps infinite) number of landing positions including its own, given that, as was asserted at the outset, his foot, whilst pointing this way, remained, like an aircraft in ordinary flight, roughly horizontal such that the point of *intersection*, to call it that, that the forward-pointing long centreline of his right foot made with the planes of the approach structure that he currently occupied was the vertical (and increasingly vertiginous) left-hand plane (from his point of view) rather than the downward angled flat plane that his left foot remained as it were planted upon.

Yet still he asserted that his right foot, from the circumscribed viewpoint described, *was*, in fact, pointing at its purported, revised, amended or altered landing position. How, though, could he maintain such a position, given it has been established that (a) the projected point of intersection of his right foot was, in fact, some (undisclosed, for now) way up the left-hand (from his point of view) wall of the increasingly vertiginous (which is to say, increasingly deep) subway-canyon; and (b) that even when considered in plan view, his foot was, in addition, pointing towards a perhaps infinite number of other landing positions in the line along which his right foot, having completed its marginal counter-clockwise swivel-in-mid-air (or thereabouts) now, as it were, pointed, which is to say in addition to the landing point that he took to be his own? The way in which he could hold this position, whilst, of course, in actuality (whatever that means), which is to say, in a bodily/physical sense continuing to move in the direction of this landing position (at least the centrepoint of the ball of his right foot continued to move towards this landing point, having, as has been established, passed the zenith of the arc that it was as it were tracing through the middle of that air), was by using the analogy of the jet-, propeller- or other type of aircraft (assuming, for now, that there are other types), as follows: just as with the aircraft of whatever type (and perhaps Zeppelins would be included in the category of aircraft) there would be a landing position that at no point in its flight it would directly point towards (in the sense that its nose would never point directly at it), so, quite simply, in the current scenario of his right foot and its purported landing position. And perhaps it was simply a question of factoring in the interplay of gravity and energy – the jet- or other aircraft, including, for now, those powered by hot air, leaving aside whether this energy source was also responsible for any forward propulsion in his investigations, could not ascend indefinitely and must, instead, *arc* through the sky such that, having programmed its co-ordinates, it could be said that it just *was*, just as in the analogous situation of his right foot, pointing at its landing position, which, he now realised, he must in fact keep as it were up in the air for as long as possible until, that is, his wheeled pursuer was at the point of passing him, so as to keep his operational parameters as open as possible in support of his investigation into the disappearance of Harold Absalon who, remember, was missing presumed dead – if, that is, he were to thwart the former's attempt to contact the woman in the tight-fitting pinstriped suit before Marguerite himself had done so, thereby keeping his investigation into that disappearance – and all that depended upon it – as it were alive.

14

THE RIDER-PROPELLED small-wheeled non-motorised vehicle continued to accelerate, presumably, down the ramp leading initially away from, and then (via a horizontal rectangular plane) towards the mouth, so-called, of the pedestrian underpass proper. What Marguerite meant to say by this, as he noticed that the woman in the tight-fitting pinstriped suit had rearranged her manicured hands in relation to Richard Knox's briefcase such that her right hand, now, was holding the left side of same as she reached, with her left, for what Marguerite presumed was the combination lock to the left of the left-hand clasp, was that the distance between it (or, more importantly, between the self propelling the self-propelled small-wheeled non-motorised vehicle) and Marguerite's own self would be decreasing increasingly quickly, and that this rapidly increasing decrease related directly to the fact that he and it (to call the self propelling itself in the manner described, which is to say using the self-propelled small-wheeled non-motorised vehicle, an 'it', for now) were both on a ramp and, perhaps most importantly, that they were both moving *down* rather than up that ramp. The rapidly increasing decrease in distance between them, then (to leave aside specifying, on this occasion, that the 'them' related to the two selves, one of which was on foot, as it's known, the other of which was propelling themselves using a self-propelled small-wheeled non-motorised vehicle for that purpose), was partially a function of that downward incline (which more succinctly could have simply been referred to as a *de*cline) and the natural force that lends itself to items in that situation when placed on such surfaces, which is to say gravity. This was not to say that gravity did not apply in the case where such items (to call them that for now) were placed on flat surfaces rather than on inclines or declines. Granted that the surface of the earth (were that to be where the action, such as it is, is, or was, taking place, as it's known) is not, as has already been established, actually flat. Were the surface of the earth actually to be flat then it is questionable, to say the least, whether gravity would, in fact, act upon it, for the simple reason, Marguerite thought, as his foot (the right) started to approach a landing position just to the left of his left foot, that gravity sort of required planets to be spherical (he thought) in order for it to act upon them. He was a little vague on the details, he realised, as he noticed that the woman in the tight-fitting pinstriped suit was leaning slightly forwards and to the *left*, now, towards the briefcase that was placed upon her right thigh, which had been raised at an angle of approximately forty-five degrees to the horizontal by the aforementioned placement of the ball of her right foot, in its high-heeled shoe, upon the dwarf wall, and the raising of that heel to that purpose, to scrutinise, Marguerite thought, the rotary numerals of the combination lock to the left of the briefcase's left-hand clasp; yet he felt sure of the conclusion, which, to express it in another way, was that, although items attracted by gravity to planets, stars, moons or other universal objects (to call them that, for now) could be of pretty much any shape whatsoever, prime examples being that of the self propelling him- or herself using a self-propelled small-wheeled non-motorised vehicle down the ramp leading to the horizontal rectangular plane (etc.), himself (which is say Marguerite) or the attractive (in a different sense) woman in the tight-fitting pinstriped suit who, Marguerite assumed, was observing the scene with increasing alarm given the forces at work and their potential disastrous consequences for Marguerite and his investigation, the planets, stars, moons or other universal objects themselves must, for whatever reason, be at least roughly spherical themselves. This was not to say that they must be perfect spheres (and, at this point, he thought, unbidden, of the orbs protruding from beneath the blouse of the woman in the tight-fitting pinstriped suit). There could, then, be protuberances upon the surface of the spherical universal objects, meaning that they should more properly be referred to, he thought, as being *roughly*, rather than perfectly, spherical. We need only look at the surface of our own planet (assuming that all those apprehending this are on the same planet) to appreciate that hillocks, valleys, crevices, crevasses (and he wasn't sure of the difference between these two – perhaps it was one of scale; he would look it up, at his earliest convenience) or even canyons need not detract from the ability of that planet to generate gravity (if that is what it does) as a means of attracting objects of whatever shape (including, as before, the perfect, gravity-defying orbs kept tantalisingly undercover by the woman, in her tight-fitting pinstriped suit) towards it. (This was not to say that spherical or roughly spherical non-universal objects were immune from its effects: balls did not only drop at puberty, would be one way of remembering this.) Suffice to say that gravity applied in the situation he found himself in and, given that the self propelling themselves upon the self-propelled small-wheeled non-motorised vehicle towards him was upon the same decline as he was, Marguerite felt sure that the distance between them would be decreasing at an increasing speed, which is to say that the former would be accelerating towards the latter, with all of the potentially tragic, decisive consequences that that could have for one or both of them, were an equal and opposite force not applied, somehow, to prevent this.

15

T HERE WAS STILL, though, of course, the possibility that the self propelling the self-propelled small-wheeled non-motorised vehicle might steer away from Marguerite at the last minute, or thereabouts, so as to avoid him and continue their descent at increasing speed such that they would contact the woman in the tight-fitting pinstriped suit before Marguerite himself had had a chance to do so. Marguerite wanted to avoid this simply because he wanted to be first to contact the woman in the tight-fitting pinstriped suit for reasons that continue to remain somewhat obscure to us, but which were, presumably, clear to Marguerite and which related to the disappearance of Harold Absalon, the Mayor's transport advisor, who was missing presumed dead. What, then, would Marguerite achieve by adapting his trajectory so that it intercepted that of the self propelling themselves on that self-propelled small-wheeled non-motorised vehicle? Did he wish to bring about an actual collision between them (in the form of the self propelling the self-propelled small-wheeled non-motorised vehicle into him, from behind, as it's known, causing injury to one or both), he wondered, as he noticed that the right hand of the woman in the tight-fitting pinstriped suit had joined her left in manipulating, he thought, the rotary numerals of the combination lock to the left of the left-hand clasp of the briefcase that was placed upon her right thigh, which had been raised at an angle of approximately forty-five degrees to the horizontal by the aforementioned placement of the ball of her right foot, in its high-heeled shoe, upon the dwarf wall, and the raising of that heel to that purpose? Or was it more that Marguerite simply wanted the person propelling themselves in the manner described (and isn't it questionable, now, given the exigencies of gravity previously expounded upon, that there was, in fact, an individual rather than an as it were celestial propellant at play; he would, no doubt, return to this theme anon[10]) to arrest their progress for themselves before that collision was as it were effected? Those were, Marguerite thought, broadly the three possibilities that could unfold for them in the immediate aftermath of his abrupt change of direction, which is to say, succinctly, overtaking, collision or deceleration; and, given his undoubted investigative expertise, it would be remiss of him not to explore, in full, as his right foot now passed to a point lower down the slope than his left without actually touching down upon that slope, their possible consequences, as well, of course, as his preferred outcome(s).

One possible consequence of option (a), which is to say of the option whereby the accelerant, to call them that, overtakes Marguerite, as it's known, without, that is, reducing their speed or rate of acceleration, this effected by them overtaking to the right rather than to the left of our investigator (as we look), would be that they would no longer be on what is known, Marguerite thought, as the racing line. This is a line, as the name implies, that those in a race wish to attain and remain on so as to (i) (and he used the lower case roman numerals here to indicate this as a sub-set of the list of options

---

10 On the desk was a brown envelope, which I surreptitiously slipped inside my jacket.

that he was currently in the process of so expertly expounding) follow the easiest fast route around that race track, thereby (ii) preventing those further behind in the race from straightforwardly overtaking them whilst following that line themselves. Marguerite thought it was something like that, at least (and note that this line was rarely actually marked on the track; rather, it was a line that those who were experienced racers would instinctively know to follow, taking a wide approach to corners being the classic example). Marguerite would, in moving to the left (as we look) so as to block the accelerant's route, be preventing the latter (and presumably also ourselves) from following that course, which, were the accelerant to be an experienced racer, they would know to be the racing line given the approach of what, in racing parlance, would, Marguerite thought, be known as a hairpin bend, due to its resemblance to an item used, predominantly by women, for the purpose implied by its name, with the resemblance relating primarily, he thought, to the tightness of the radii in both instances. The main consequence of this for Marguerite's investigation, in the situation where the accelerant continued to accelerate, would be an increased risk of collision either with Marguerite (which, remember, was scenario (b) – a scenario that Marguerite would, presumably, come on to presently) or with the walls that so precipitously lined both ramps (which is to say the current ramp, so-called, which, remember led away from the mouth of the pedestrian underpass proper, and the ramp that led, and/or leads, down towards it) as well as the horizontal rectangular plane connecting them. And it was this very risk, Marguerite thought, that would bring about scenario (c) – Marguerite's preferred outcome – which was the scenario, remember, in which the accelerant actually *decelerated* (and the prospect of this immediately flagged to Marguerite how ill-judged the nomenclature had been until now) to such an extent that they would come to an abrupt stop behind Marguerite and, in this scenario, either incline the front wheels of their rider-propelled small-wheeled non-motorised vehicle and then take it up into their arms (in the case where that non-motorised vehicle was what's known as a skateboard) or, in the case where the rider-propelled small-wheeled non-motorised vehicle was what's known as a scooter (non-motorised, as implied by both the 'self-propelled' and 'non-motorised' qualifiers as well, perhaps, as the 'small-wheeled' one), they would, presumably, continue to wheel it whilst placing both feet directly upon the incline so as to walk (in all cases) at a similar or slower pace to Marguerite's so as to avoid colliding with him or with the walls that so precipitously contained the space that they were descending through. That this latter outcome, which was preferred by Marguerite, might not be the one that came to pass was evidenced by the fact that there was nothing, yet, to suggest that the sounds emanating from the accelerant would necessitate any change of name on their part.

16

THE CONTINUED ACCELERATION behind him might be indicative, he now realised, of the class of rider-propelled small-wheeled non-motorised vehicle containing roller-skates or -blades (a category he'd included in the original family of small-wheeled non-motorised vehicles before promptly, it would seem, discounting them), with the increased manoeuvrability afforded by objects within this class perhaps fatally undermining his previous contention that, were he to occupy what's known as the racing line, this would cause the accelerant either to stop abruptly behind him or to collide with him or with the walls that lined that ramped cavern leading down to the pedestrian underpass proper which spanned that broad tree-lined avenue with a row of showrooms on one side of it and a vast expanse of parkland on the other, with the manoeuvrability being a function, quite simply, he thought, of the deployment of these conveyances invariably as a pair – one for each foot – such that they can be used at varying angles to one another. On reflection, however, he had been wrong to include roller-skates/blades in the category of small-wheeled self-propelled non-motorised vehicle in the first place – not, of course, because they were motorised (typically), were ordinarily anything other than rider-propelled or had large wheels, but, quite simply, because he took it to be self-evident that human-powered conveyances that are only ever deployed as a pair should not, by definition, be classified as vehicles.

Why this concern with plurality, he now wondered, turning, in his mind only (note) directly to it, as he heard a scraping sound directly behind him? After all, wasn't the category of 'non-motorised vehicle' clear, distinct and perfectly accommodating, by definition, of all those devices designed as human-propelled conveyances – of self, other, cargo (broadly defined) or of trash? But it was not in that way that he had meant it, he now realised, as he noticed that the woman in the tight-fitting pinstriped suit was no longer leaning slightly forwards and to the left. How, then, had he meant it, he wondered, as, he concluded that she had, at last, entered the correct combination and opened, with her left hand, the briefcase's *left*-hand clasp? A review of those objects that he had hitherto placed within the category of small-wheeled non-motorised vehicle would, he thought, assist him: skateboard, non-motorised scooter, wheeled suitcase, pushchair, transport wheelchair, parcel trolley, hand cart, trolley-bag, pram, stroller, meals on wheels and wheelie bin. What was it that these had that roller-skates/blades lacked? Or, rather, what was it that the latter lacked that was obtained, in contrast, by the former? He realised that what he had meant when he'd originally formed the category of non-motorised vehicle was that it should only contain items that resembled motorised vehicles but which were not, in fact, motorised. In other words, he had not meant the term 'non-motorised vehicle' to encompass all human-propelled conveyances but had instead intended it to be defined as a sub-set of those conveyances that, whilst being non-motorised, did, in fact, resemble their motorised counterparts in some crucial way. Clearly, then, the best route through this impasse would be to identify the ways in which those conveyances that he had included within the list of 'non-motorised vehicles' (as originally, implicitly, defined) resembled what some thought of as vehicles proper and contrast this with those objects that he now excluded from that category. He would, in other words, pursuant to this inquiry, identify for us those characteristics of the list of non-motorised vehicles that qualified them to be included within that category, and contrast this with the equivalent characteristics of the as it were non-motorised non-vehicles, were those characteristics to exist (and their absence might, of course, be the very reason for their disqualification from the category in question), as a means of demonstrating why the latter (which is to say the so-called non-motorised non-vehicles) could not be included within that category (of non-motorised vehicle)".

What, then, were the characteristics of the non-motorised vehicles (as originally, implicitly, defined) that enabled them to be referred to in this way? In other words, in what ways did the non-motorised vehicles resemble their motorised counterparts? He would take the non-freight variety first, and say that one characteristic of same was that these non-motorised vehicles, like vehicles proper, tended to have three (in the case of most self-propelled scooters) or four (in the case of all skateboards and a sub-set of self-propelled scooters) wheels. They also had a steering mechanism of some sort – a rudimentary handlebar in the case of the self-propelled scooter, and a tilting mechanism in the case of the skateboard. Contrast this with the equivalent characteristics of the non-motorised non-vehicles in the form of roller-skates/-blades and you may obtain a modicum, at least, of satisfaction, in that the latter

---

11 I found it to contain expense receipts for a hotel stay in the name of Harold Absalon, a former Knox protégé who had disappeared following a sordid extra-marital affair with a colleague.

tended to consist of more than four wheels (in total, per pair – an important and somewhat undermining caveat this) and did not tend to have a steering mechanism (at least in the case of rollerblades – some roller-*skates* did, in fact, have rudimentary steering, as he understood it (having never tried a pair), thereby undermining this aspect of his inquiry still further). Furthermore (and this would hopefully clinch it, given the preceding questionable reasoning) the non-motorised vehicles proper tended to be larger than the non-motorised non-vehicles (although not, of course, to the extent that they approached the scale of vehicles proper).

What then, of those non-motorised vehicles designed to carry goods or trash, he wondered, as he noticed that the woman in the tight-fitting pinstriped suit was finally opening the briefcase, which is to say that she had raised the lid of same such that it subtended an increasing angle in relation to the remainder thereof? Perhaps these would be so clear and distinct from the category of non-motorised non-vehicle, and so resemble the members of the category of vehicles proper that it would settle this now long-running argument once and for all. But what he noticed, immediately, was that, if anything, these non-motorised vehicles, taken together, resembled vehicles even less than the non-vehicles used primarily to propel people in that they (the parcel trolley or wheeled suitcase, for instance) resembled vehicle *trailers* (whether forward- or, as it were rear-facing) far more than they resembled vehicles proper, with the human in question providing the transmission rather than the lorry cab or the train engine, say (although in some instances, such as the goods-train or -lorry, it could be argued that the trailer is, at least, *part* of the vehicle proper).

Frustrated at the proliferating nature of this branch of his inquiry, he resolved to continue to pursue it at his leisure, were he ever to experience any in his pursuit of Harold Absalon, the Mayor's transport advisor, who was missing presumed dead, given that what had turned into a prolonged scraping sound had, now, stopped and was immediately succeeded by a loud slap directly behind and to one side of him.

17

THE SCRAPING REMAINED undefined (although Marguerite continued to have his speculations and suspicions about what it consisted in), but the slap inarguably must have come from the soles of shoes of some sort abruptly hitting the paving slabs behind and to one side of him in a circumstance not unlike that involving what is known as an ejector seat. This was a seat that ejected itself, as the name implies, under certain circumstances, which is to say, ejected itself in an emergency typically entailing (a) a jet-fighter or other aircraft having been shot down, or – Marguerite's favoured scenario – a fast-moving sports car heading irrevocably towards a cliff or other precipitous drop, and heading, moreover, towards the edge, rather than the base, of that cliff or other precipitous drop (although similar, but perhaps somewhat less dramatic consequences might follow from the latter scenario or sub-scenario) such that the occupant(s) of that car would, were they not to eject themselves abruptly in the manner described, risk serious injury or, more likely, death, given their encasement (with or without seatbelt(s)) within that vehicle, which must, for what Marguerite hoped were obvious reasons, be what's known as convertible, or, at least, be partially convertible, a vehicle, remember, that is already travelling at speed, a speed that would be added to, as it were, through the aforementioned effects of gravity, but with the added issue of having no way of arresting one's trajectory once one was as it were airborne (since air brakes, despite the name, were not designed for that purpose), with the ejector seat(s) presumably also including within them parachutes that would automatically and swiftly open upon ejection, this being the form that brakes take in that case, which is to say, parachutes being the form par excellence of reducing one's speed during a fall, a speed that would otherwise of course, through the effects of you-know-what, continue to increase until a terminal (in more ways than one) velocity had been reached; or (b) the situation in which one had a person in one's sports car that one no longer wanted to spend time with, in which case one could either eject oneself (this in the case, usually, when for complicated reasons, one wanted to terminate that person's life, with this eventuality occurring through the simple action of not ejecting their seat when one ejected one's own, in the precarious situation in which that speeding (remember) sports car found itself within) or one could eject the other person (in the situation in which one was perhaps enjoying the drive, wanting to continue, or in which one treasured one's sports car – not unusual this – to the extent that one was reluctant to give it up, if one could help it, by ejecting oneself, which, given one was likely to be literally and metaphorically in the driving seat[12] might inevitably, given the situation under consideration, lead to the destruction of that prized possession and its remaining occupant(s), who, presumably, would be less prized for reasons already hinted at) although one wonders why one would put oneself in a situation in which one wanted to eject oneself or one's passenger during such a drive – would it not have been better to have been more discerning about one's passenger(s) at the outset, Marguerite wondered, as he

12 An accompanying note read, simply, 'Find'.

felt a sudden sharp pain in his rear left-side torso?

Typically there was, or were, no passenger(s) in the case of the rider-propelled small-wheeled non-motorised vehicle of course, in which case the similarity must be one in which one, as the as it were sole pilot of a member of the sub-category of such non-motorised vehicles whereby one propelled oneself using one's feet (this sub-set precluding roller-skates/-blades given their disqualification, to Marguerite's mind, as non-motorised non-vehicles) in such a way that one or more of those feet (up to a maximum of a pair) could, at speed, be ejected, or eject itself/themselves from that vehicle in an emergency, for instance, such as in a situation in which someone placed themselves in the direct path of that speeding rider-propelled small-wheeled non-motorised vehicle in the way that Marguerite had done, and, in so doing, shortly thereafter hit the pavement/sidewalk/ramp down towards (etc.) a pedestrian underpass that spanned a broad tree-lined avenue with a row of showrooms on one side of it and a vast expanse of parkland on the other, in such a way as invariably to produce the abrupt auditory signifier commonly identified, through its similarity with what at a particular point in history had been the favoured physical strike of wife against husband[13] (but *not*, typically, note, vice versa – or not often), as a slap. It must, then, exist, this small-wheeled non-motorised vehicle (the sound of which, Marguerite noticed, had now resumed behind and to the right of him), in the sub-category of such small wheeled non-motorised vehicles in which (a) one of the requisite pair of feet was employed in propulsion, if only to

13 There was, then, someone else within the project team with information. The thing I found most strange was that the handwriting on the accompanying note most resembled Hazel's.

generate the initial acceleration which was then subsequently sustained, in the case where the non-motorised vehicle was, as it were, travelling downhill, as in the case under examination here, by the normal action of gravity, as previously discussed; and (b) one or more, up to the requisite pair, of those feet must be free to eject themselves, under certain circumstances, such that it/they would hit the surface of that hill (so-called) at sufficient speed, and at an angle that was equal, or near-equal, to that of the surface such that it or they resembled the more or less flat palm of a wife's hand as it approached, at a similar angle, the undoubtedly more curved cheek of the husband and perhaps at a similar level of acceleration to the extent that the former produced an abrupt deviation in the local ambient air pressure that would transmit itself to those in its vicinity in the form of a sound wave which, once apprehended and as it were cognitively processed, many would subsume under the term applied to the latter, which is to say, the slap. It excluded, in short, those types of human self-propulsion wherein the feet (as before) were strapped or otherwise fastened to a small-wheeled conveyance, such as roller-skates/-blades (whose users he now categorised as small-wheeled non-motorised *pedestrians*); it also excluded from its purview those non-motorised vehicles that did not use the feet (etc.) as the main form of propulsion, which is to say, that category of small-wheeled human-powered conveyance in which one of the requisite pair of feet is placed *upon* it as the primary means of its propulsion, with the other foot using the friction inherent (or designed into) the upper surface of that small-wheeled conveyance to press forwards against that surface as the very means of (initial or ongoing) propulsion.

This, then, was what Marguerite had surmised: that the

slap was that of a foot, or feet, being ejected from the surface of a rider-propelled small-wheeled non-motorised vehicle and hitting the ramp of the pedestrian underpass behind and to one side of him at such force and, of course, at an angle that was equal or near-equal to that of the ramp itself, that it produced what Marguerite and, no doubt, any other astute and attentive individuals in the vicinity with the necessary perceptual apparatus had/would have referred to, immediately, as a slap – this, he thought, as a means of effecting an emergency stop immediately behind him, an action that he had precipitated by his abrupt traverse (when viewed, somehow, from above) manoeuvre on that ramp. That this so-called slap had been directly succeeded by a sharp pain in his rear left-side torso, which he took to have been caused by what's known as a handlebar (strictly in the singular, to Marguerite's mind) contacting that area at speed, suggested to him that, rather than belonging, as it were, to the sub-class of rider-propelled small-wheeled non-motorised vehicle that was enduringly popular, particularly in the urban areas of the city that he frequented, which was the skateboard, he deduced that the noises must have emanated from a more recent, but no less widely deployed, sub-class or sub-sub-class of such surface-mounted, foot-propelled non-motorised vehicle – and this was his least favourite within that sub-class or sub-sub-class: the rider-propelled small-wheeled non-motorised vehicle commonly referred to as the scooter.

18

M ARGUERITE BROUGHT HIS left foot into play,
now: this being the logical next step, which is to say
that given he had most recently used his right foot in furtherance of his forward propulsion it would seem logical, would
it not, in the case of a biped such as himself, to bring the left
foot into play, as it were, immediately after this? He did not
actually want to bring the left foot into play at this juncture,
however, for reasons he would come on to. But bring it into
play he nevertheless did; and the way in which he brought it
into play, as the woman in the tight-fitting pinstriped suit
starting rifling around in the briefcase, was by lifting the
toes of that foot, the heel already being in the air, given the
extension in that limb brought about by the placement of the
right foot, as a precursor to removing that left foot entirely
from the ramp leading initially away from, but ultimately,
via a horizontal rectangular plane, towards, the mouth of the
pedestrian underpass proper, and placing it, he hoped, to the
right, note, of the right foot (which was, remember, still, to
the left of the left foot, for reasons previously adumbrated),
given that it was from this side, remember (which is to say, the
right side from Marguerite's and, presumably, somehow, our
point of view), that the sound of small wheels on flagstones
was now, once again, emanating. This, then, was the reason
that, despite it being the logical next step he did not wish to
make that step but was compelled to do so by the dynamic

unfolding before (and behind) him in his investigation into the disappearance of Harold Absalon, the Mayor's transport advisor, who was missing presumed dead. In other words, were he to wish to place his left foot to the left of a right foot that was currently to the left of that left foot then he would take that step with alacrity; given, though, that he wished to place his left foot to the *right* of a right foot that was currently to the left of that left foot meant that it was with reluctance that he would take this step, even though he could not deny that it was the logical one. And the reason he wished to place his left foot to the right of a right foot that was currently to the left of that left foot related to the fact that the person behind him had re-boarded their scooter with the intention, as far as Marguerite could judge by the auditory signals emanating from that scooter (in the broad sense of vehicle and/or rider, viz, 'one who scoots'), to pass him to the right, which is to say that the scooter (in the latter sense) intended, so far as Marguerite could intuit, to pass to Marguerite's right, having initially intended, Marguerite thought, to pass to his left, and, since Marguerite wished to prevent the scooter from passing him on either side, if he could help it, he, which is to say Marguerite, would need to move in the direction towards which he adjudged the scooter to be moving as a precursor to passing Marguerite, which in the current instance was to Marguerite's right, as previously stated, and it was for this reason that Marguerite must move to that side, which is to say, to his (own) right-hand side, despite the fact that his as it were active foot was his left foot, meaning that he would have to move that foot to that side, which is to say that he would have to move his left foot to the right of a right foot that was actually, at that moment (still) to the left of that left foot, and, in so doing, move that left foot right around his right leg given that that leg was blocking a more direct route for that left foot. He would, in short, move a left foot that was already, in fact, to the right of that right foot, although behind it, to a location further, note, to the right of that right foot, and marginally in front of it, thereby preventing the scooter from passing him on that side, just as Marguerite had previously prevented the same scooter from passing him on the other side, which is to say on Marguerite's left, by a similar manoeuvre towards that side, which is to say by moving his right foot, in that case, right around his left foot and then placing that right foot as far to the left of that foot as anatomically possible as a means of moving his body (the remainder thereof) in the same direction so as to block the person scooting from scooting, or passing him in some other way such as walking on that side, even though the right foot, in that previous instance, had started this manoeuvre from a more natural location, which is to say that it had started this manoeuvre from a position adjacent to, and in advance of, the left foot, with this adjacency being, crucially, to the right of that left foot rather than to the left of it, as was the case in the current scenario, although the positions were, of course, reversed in the latter, as it were, live, instance. It was for this and other subsidiary reasons, which is to say that it was for this reason and for other subsidiary reasons, that Marguerite took this logical, metaphorical and actual next step, despite his reluctance to do so; rather, he took the next metaphorical step in furtherance of this next actual step, which was finally to remove those left toes, which is to say the toes of his left foot rather than the leftmost toes of his right, from the angled (downwards) surface as a precursor, this, to that foot's flight around the right leg and its placement below (given the incline), and in advance and to the right of, which is to say below (etc.), in advance and to the right of, the right foot as a method of preventing the scooter from passing him on that side and thwarting his investigation into the disappearance of Harold Absalon, the Mayor's transport advisor, who was missing presumed dead, which he felt he was now on the verge of solving.

19

A ND WHAT HE found, as he removed the toes of his
left foot not from the remainder of that foot, for that
would have added to the excruciating pain that he was already
feeling in his body, but from the downward incline that was
the ramp upon which all of this action, so-called, is taking
place, as a precursor, remember, to placing that foot as far to
the right of his right foot as he could muster, anatomically
speaking, was that the nose of a *skateboard* rather than a
scooter had entered the bottom right quadrant of his peripheral vision, which is to say that the front end of a skateboard
had entered the periphery of his vision such that he took that
skateboard to be located on that decline in a position next to,
and just to the right of, his left foot, although he took it as a
given that the skateboard was not, in fact, stationary adjacent
to that foot. And the pressing questions that entered his mind
(and therefore, by extension, somehow, this report) at that
moment were (i) how had this scenario come to pass, which is
to say, how had his reasoning once again been so flawed as to
misclassify the rider-propelled small-wheeled non-motorised
vehicle, and at such a crucial stage of his investigation into
the disappearance of Harold Absalon, the Mayor's transport
advisor, who was missing presumed dead, such that it put his
own life in jeopardy; (ii) what had caused the sharp pain in
his rear left-side torso, given the lack of handlebar on this particular form of rider-propelled small-wheeled non-motorised

vehicle, which is to say, on the skateboard; and (iii) had the person who'd hitherto been using that skateboard to propel themselves, assisted, as we know, by force of gravity, down that ramp that intercepted the horizontal rectangular plane towards which the woman in the tight-fitting pinstriped suit would, he hoped, soon also be trajected, re-established physical contact with it – had the skateboarder re-boarded, in other words, by placing one or more (to, as before, a maximum of two) of their feet upon that board, or had the board as it were decisively broken the connection with its owner, in fact, such that it was now roaming free, which is to say that it was now rolling downwards, under force of gravity, towards that horizontal rectangular plane upon which so much seemed about to coalesce, with this latter scenario, which Marguerite immediately dubbed 'free-board', offering up to him, if he could play it well, a more favourable possibility of progression, both literally and, as before, metaphorically, in his investigation into the disappearance of Harold Absalon, the Mayor's transport advisor, who was missing presumed dead, in that it would offer him the opportunity to mount that board and use it to propel himself much more speedily than was the case under his current means of propulsion – the usual bipedic perambulation – towards that horizontal rectangular plane and thence into the arms, as it's known, of the woman in the tight-fitting pinstriped suit? Regardless, though, of whether the rider had re-boarded in this way, Marguerite knew that he must mount that skateboard were his investigation into the disappearance of Harold Absalon, the Mayor's transport advisor, who was missing presumed dead, not to be thwarted at this critical juncture. It was for this reason, then, that he inclined his head downwards, slightly, and to the right, slightly, as a means of bringing the nose of that skateboard more fully into the central rather than a peripheral portion of his vision, this so as to better judge how to effect the placement of his left foot, which was, after all, the one that was in airborne motion, upon the top of what must, now, be an accelerating small-wheeled rider-propelled or freewheeling (as it's known) non-motorised vehicle, which is to say, an accelerating small-wheeled non-motorised vehicle that was either occupied or unoccupied and, in the former scenario, was either rider-propelled or freewheeling, and in the latter was *ipso facto* freewheeling, with Marguerite's name, as it were, all over it.

20

T H E   N O S E   O F   the skateboard which Marguerite could
see in more, now, than just the lower-rightmost extent
of his peripheral vision was, of course, pointing down the
incline as it continued to roll down the same. And the manner
in which the downwards-pointing skateboard was rolling
down that incline related, of course, to its wheels rather
than its board as it were, such that, were its nose not to
be pointing down the incline down which the erstwhile (or
current) boarder was also, perhaps, descending, along with
ourselves (presumably; and Marguerite (etc.)), then it could
not, Marguerite thought, be asserted that the way in which
it was rolling down that decline related to its wheels rather
than its board. And what he meant to express by this, as his
left foot moved around towards the rear of his right leg, was
that were the nose of the board to be pointing in a direction
other than forwards then it could not as it were make use of
the ordinary function of the wheels in propelling it in that
direction; it would, in other words, have to roll in a different
fashion, laterally rather than longitudinally, so to speak, such
that the long edges of the board would alternately and repeatedly be in contact with that surface (which, as we know, is a
decline in the specific circumstances unfolding before us, with
the 'us' again being of an inclusive nature in that it included
Marguerite within its compass) as would the lower edge of the
four wheels with which the board formed an integral whole,

a whole to which, typically, one applied the label 'skateboard' despite the fact that this label made no allusion whatsoever to the presence within that whole of the aforementioned wheels. In other words, were we to view the skateboard, as typically defined, from behind (and some of us may be in a position to do so, even if Marguerite is not, given our position in relation to him, which is to say, following, presumably, more or less in his footsteps[14]) and, from this position, were to draw a circle that included, within its circumference, the four aforementioned (which is to say the afourmentioned) points (namely the topmost longitudinal edges of the board proper, and the bottommost outer edges of the afourmentioned wheels (although we would only be able to see two of same given our as it were end-on view)) then it would be these four points (or, granted, edges, when viewed from any other angle aside from rear- or front-on), which is to say the afourmentioned points upon the circumference of that circle, that would be in touch with the surface in question, which, in our case (this now including Marguerite again, despite this end-on viewing not lending itself to his current location in relation to the board in question), is, of course, the decline leading down to, and intersecting with, the horizontal rectangular plane towards which the woman in the tight-fitting pinstriped suit would also soon, we hope, be heading; and the skateboard, were it to be rolling down that decline in the manner described, which is to say, quite succinctly, now, lengthwise, then not only would it be making quite a lot more noise, and a different sort of noise from the noise it was currently making in

---

14 She had worked under Knox for years, and I suspected there had been a sexual element to their relationship, but could not be sure. How, then, could I be certain she was no longer loyal to him?

rolling down the decline through the contact of the whole of the circumference of the aforementioned wheels and the axial revolution of same, but it could also be quite safely asserted in this instance that no-one was riding it. It would also not, Marguerite thought, be rolling in such a speedy and sustained fashion as it was currently doing, nose-first, such that he feared his left foot would not attain the surface thereof in a way that would propel him, he hoped, straight into the arms, as it's known, of the woman in the tight-fitting pinstriped suit and, beyond that, to a solution to this painstaking investigation into the disappearance of Harold Absalon, the Mayor's transport advisor, who continued, as far as we know, to be missing presumed dead.

21

HOW, THEN, WOULD he manage to land a foot on this particular moving target? Or, speaking metaphorically, momentarily, how could he land this particular jet-fighter upon that particular aircraft carrier? Both foot and board were moving, and the trick, if there was one, would be to try and ensure that the former's movements mimicked the latter's until the two could as it were be coupled. This was a situation, remember, unlike the ordinary in that the standing foot (the right in this instance) was some distance from the board in question with the other foot, having been immediately adjacent to the board, now needing to travel all around the headland that was as it were formed by the right leg in seeking to land upon the upper surface, which is to say the upward-*facing* surface, of that board. Marguerite intimated from the foregoing that at a particular key moment, and at a location that might properly be called a fulcrum, that his left foot would need to commence a reverse arc as it started to follow the trajectory of the manned or unmanned skateboard in its onwards downward journey, which is to say an arc that was the mirror image of that currently being traced by his left foot around a right leg that also as it were belonged to him (and not merely as some prized possession but as a constituent and not unimportant or peripheral part of his body) as it continued its asymptotic pursuit of the freewheeling, so-called, or rider-propelled skateboard to his right, with the purpose of this transition being to enable that left foot to be in a position to as it were couple[15] with that skateboard, which is to say to be in a position to land securely upon its upper surface whilst displacing any rider (of any gender) from the same surface without impeding the onward downward motion such that he could utilise the momentum of that board to his advantage by using it to propel him downward into the arms, as it's known, of the woman in the tight-fitting pinstriped suit who was, he thought, at pains to help him in his investigation into the disappearance of Harold Absalon, the Mayor's transport advisor, who was missing presumed dead.

The point might be expressed more succinctly with the assistance of the letter 'S', although this is an 'S' that is both flipped on its vertical axis and rotated counter-clockwise around what Marguerite had previously referred to as the fulcrum. In still other, perhaps less abstract words, it could be said, Marguerite thought, as his left foot moved around the rear of his right leg, that whereas the left foot was currently involved in as it were sketching a circle in a clockwise trajectory through the air (whether thin or otherwise) around the right leg, it would, at a certain as yet unidentified point, transition from this clockwise sketching to a counter-clockwise sketching, and the numerical figure-of-eight may assist more, in fact, than the inverse swivelled 'S' so long as we also swivel that figure clockwise or anticlockwise by ninety degrees from its traditional numeric orientation so that it is lying more or less flat and don't assume that Marguerite's left foot would complete the whole figure. The point, in short,

15 It came as no surprise to me when, a few days later, having followed my preferred route down the back stairs and along the corridor that led past the print- and post-rooms, the electrical intake panel and the showers, I encountered Hazel herself down in the archive.

towards which he was approaching, realising, in fact that this figure: ∞, which is to say the figure for infinity should, in fact, supersede the figures previously tendered to us for the simple reason that it required no reorientation in order for us (or Marguerite, rather) to use it, which, given how much Marguerite and his body (and bodily senses) were involved in could be nothing other than an advantage (this assuming that we are, as so often, applying this figure from a God's eye view, which is to say in plan, from above, regardless of whether we have theological leanings or not), was that the left foot, having commenced its movement around the fulcrum that was the right leg in a clockwise direction, would need, at a key moment, which is to say when it had, in fact, passed the location of the right leg and was on the same side of it as its starting position, to commence a *counter*-clockwise revolution around a point equidistant from the centre of that figure and the closest point on the longitudinal centreline of the freewheeling (occupied or unoccupied) or rider-propelled skateboard, to enable that left foot to approach that skateboard in a position and at a velocity such that it could mount the upward-facing board of same whilst displacing any rider and simultaneously maintaining the momentum of that skateboard at that point so as to utilise it in his (which is to say, in Marguerite's) forward motion towards the horizontal rectangular landing plane and thence, he hoped, towards the woman in the tight-fitting pinstriped suit, who, he noticed, had retrieved, with her right hand, a small round metal case from inside the briefcase, with this manoeuvre of that left foot around that fulcrum and then around the equidistant point being best described – or depicted, rather, symbolically – by the aforementioned figure for infinity.

This, then, was the figure that he alighted upon as his foot continued tracing its outline, realising, in that moment, that, in moving through its central point, which he hoped eventually to do, before landing on the upward-facing surface of that occupied or unoccupied skateboard, that he would, at that moment *ipso facto* transition from sketching more or less a circle, through air of whatever thickness, in a clockwise direction around a pivot formed by his as it were anchored right leg, to sketching more or less a circle, through air presumably of a not dissimilar thickness but in a *counter*-clockwise direction around a floating point (that is, not around the fulcrum or pivot that was the right leg), a circle, this latter, that he hoped would, at its lateral extreme, which is to say at its rightmost point, land seamlessly upon the upper surface of that skateboard (which, all this time had continued to roll down the decline in the manner previously described), without, note, having approached that point asymptotically, he realised, as the woman in the tight-fitting pinstriped suit transferred the small round metal case to her left hand, which she was also using to hold open the lid of the briefcase, in that this would imply, in fact, strictly speaking, that it would never actually attain that point but would continue to approach it indefinitely (which is, of course, tidily enough, given the symbol that was ultimately as it were alighted upon, to say that it would require an infinite elapsement of time in which to do so) and this was something that he, and no doubt we, wished to avoid given the pressing nature of his investigation into the disappearance of Harold Absalon, the Mayor's transport advisor, who was still, so far as we can tell, yet to be definitively located.

22

H E REALISED THAT once his left foot had traced that partial figure-of-eight partially revolved, which is to say revolved through ninety degrees such that it lay lengthways rather than standing, as it were, upright, then his right foot must follow suit, as it's known, which is to say that his right foot must follow the outline that the left had followed even if it did so shortly after the latter had completed its journey. Why, though, did he think that his right foot must, in time, trace the same figure, more or less, through air of whatever thickness that the left was still, note, in the process of tracing? Why, moreover, had he reverted to referring to this figure as a figure-of-eight, whether partially revolved or not, rather than as the infinity sign, the dramatic conclusion, remember, of what he, of course, could not, for reasons he chose not to or was unable to go into, think of as the previous chapter?

The answer to the first question related, he thought, to the speed of the skateboard that continued down the slope beside him, which is to say that it related to the speed of the skateboard moving under its own steam, as it were, or propelled, still, by a rider beside him down the slope that hitherto, and ongoingly, he, and it, had been descending and continued to descend, which is to say that it depended upon the speed of the skateboard that he was following or mirroring in its movement down the slope leading to the landing point – or plane, rather – towards which the woman in the tight-fitting pinstriped suit, who, he noticed, had now opened the small round metal case with her right hand whilst keeping the brief-case open with her left, would, he hoped, also eventually head, as it's known, albeit by other means, which is to say that it depended upon the speed of the skateboard that, like himself, was upon a decline leading towards that horizontal rectangular plane and was, moreover, moving down that decline, as was implied by the speculation as to the skateboard's speed, which is to say, in addition, that it depended upon the *relative* speed of that left foot through the air compared to the (gathering, remember) speed of the skateboard moving down the slope towards that horizontal rectangular plane, which Marguerite had been referring to, pretty consistently he thought, as the landing point (and there's the rub) for both himself and for the woman in the tight-fitting pinstriped suit, with that point not being exactly the same for both of them, a problem he hoped to rectify by moving from that point, having negotiated the landing successfully, to a point immediately adjacent to that woman's landing point or in the case where that woman had moved to another location within, or outside of, that horizontal rectangular plane, to a position immediately adjacent to *that* point, which is to say that it depended upon the speed of his left foot relative to the speed of the occupied or unoccupied skateboard moving down the slope beside him, a final, for now, formulation that he would have to live with given the pressing nature of his investigation into the disappearance of Harold Absalon, the Mayor's transport advisor, who was missing presumed dead (which is not to prejudge the possibility of Harold Absalon having actually been found by the time you read this). And the reason that the answer to the first question, which is to say, the question of why he thought that his right foot must, in time, trace more or less the figure, however that figure is referred to, that the left was in the process of tracing (and note that the left would, in fact, imminently pass through the westernmost point of that revolved partial '8' or non-revolved non-inverted partial '∞', which is to say, the location, on its route, that was furthest from its projected landing position upon the upward-facing surface of that occupied or unoccupied skateboard), depended upon the speed of his left foot in relation to that of the skateboard, a foot that would, by then, be at the same angle, and would be moving in the same direction and at an identical speed to the skateboard, related to where this would leave the right foot in relation to that skateboard since, were the skateboard to be travelling at low speed, then it might be that the left foot, when attaining its surface - like a jet landing on an aircraft carrier having, as it were, flown around a headland which in Marguerite's case was represented by his right leg planted via an angled right foot upon the incline down which the skateboard continued to move at an as yet still undisclosed but ever increasing speed, but without the assistance of the elasticated band stretched laterally across it such that it engaged a hook at the rear of that jet to dramatically arrest its speed so as to bring it to what is known as a standstill - would still be adjacent to, but on the other side, of course, of the right leg, and what he meant by this was that, if the skateboard was travelling slowly enough for it still to be beside him, to the right, when his left foot finally made contact with it (without, remember, the assistance of any on-board elasticated arrest mechanism), which, given its speed relative to that foot, he envisaged would indeed be the case, then his other foot, which is to say his right, would by (verbal) extension be roughly adjacent to that board and to his left foot, which, as we know, would, by now, have been placed upon it (which is to say upon the surface of that occupied or unoccupied skateboard) such that its position would be remarkably similar to, although the inverse of, the starting position of that left foot, which would, by then, have travelled through air of whatever thickness around the so-called headland formed by the right leg to land upon the surface of that skateboard, which continued to move down that slope towards that ecstatic (he hoped) mutual landing point. And it was the very fact that the starting position of the right foot under these circumstances (which, mercifully, he refrained from re-adumbrating on this occasion) would be the mirror image, to put it in that way (with the mirror located, note, between his legs and aligned such that it was parallel to the walls of the approach to the pedestrian underpass proper, which were of increasing height and were on either, which is to say on both, side(s) of him), of what had been the starting point of his left foot under similar circumstances that had led him to conclude that that foot (the right) would follow its immediate predecessor in tracing what he had intermittently reverted to calling a partially revolved partial figure-of-eight for the simple reason, to address the second question now, in the time remaining, that it lent itself more easily, even with the angular modifications required, to verbal, rather than the symbolic expression necessitated, he thought, as his left foot passed the seam that, as it were, ran down the left side of his right-side trouser leg, by what he referred to, in conclusion, now, as the other two still-elegant forms.

23

I T H A S T O be said, though, as the left foot continued around the headland formed by the right leg, that in mirroring the movements, through air of whatever thickness, of its counterpart, to call it that, which is to say of this very left foot, the right foot would not, assuming that it was headed for the same destination, which is to say the upward-facing surface of the freewheeling (occupied or unoccupied) or rider-propelled skateboard to Marguerite's right, fully replicate, to call it that, the trajectory of that counterpart in that, whereas the left foot, in attaining that same surface, which is to say the upward-facing surface of the freewheeling (occupied or unoccupied) or rider-propelled skateboard to Marguerite's right, would have accomplished a complete, or near-complete, circumnavigation of its *own* counterpart (which is to say the right leg), given that it had started and would, in fact, end up, as it's known, to the right of that right leg, the right foot, in mirroring or replicating the movements of its counterpartial predecessor, to call it that now, would only, he thought, as his left foot passed, now, onto the arc of the quadrant bounded by the seam that, as it were, ran down the left of his right-side trouser leg and the crease that, as it were, ran down the front of same, complete a partial – and perhaps he could be more specific, here: a less than three-quarters yet more than a half – circumnavigation of that predecessor, not only because it, which is to say, the left foot, would have preceded its counterpart (etc.) in landing upon the freewheeling (occupied or unoccupied) or rider-propelled skateboard, which would have continued its forward (and downward) trajectory to the extent, he now estimated, that it, which is to say (again), the left foot, would decisively and definitively be in front, and to the right, note[16], of that counterpart, but also because the right foot, having completed its partial, which is to say, less than three-quarters yet more than a half, circumnavigation of its counterpartial predecessor, to call the left foot that again, would, then, in fact, land on the surface that would already have been attained by his left foot – the upward-facing surface of that freewheeling (occupied or unoccupied) or rider-propelled skateboard, remember – in advance, which is to say, in front of, same, despite Marguerite being what's known as right-footed, whereas the left foot, given its speed relative to that skateboard and the consequent position of the latter when the former made contact with it (viz., still to the right, but *not* in front, of its counterpartial successor, to call the right foot that now) would, unlike that right foot, have accomplished a complete, or near-complete, circumnavigation of its predecessor before also, of course, completing a partial figure-of-eight by completing the partial counter-clockwise circumnavigation of a point equidistant from the centre of that figure and the closest point on the longitudinal centreline of the freewheeling (occupied or unoccupied) or rider-propelled skateboard, which was why he had asserted that the circumnavigation in question, which his right foot was still some way from embarking upon given that its predecessor was still passing through the quadrant bounded

16 She'd laid out cartons of takeaway food at my usual makeshift workspace in a corner behind one of the document stacks. 'We don't want you wasting away,' she said, and I was ecstatic. I indicated with a hand gesture that she should join me, but she demurred.

by the seam that, as it were, ran down the left of his right-side trouser leg and the crease that, as it were, ran down the front of same, would, unlike this complete-, or near-complete-, circumnavigation performed by his left foot around the right leg, be a partial and, more specifically, a greater than two- and less than three-quartile, circumnavigation given that he wanted that latter partial (as before) circumnavigation to end directly, or thereabouts, in front of (although, for this reason, it would also, for what he hoped were obvious reasons, be *below*) that left foot on the aforementioned upward-facing surface, despite him being what's known as right-footed, and leaving aside, for now, and perhaps forever, the confusing, perhaps even contradictory combination of the metaphorical concepts 'headland' (potentially implying, he thought, navigation, but certainly not *circum*navigation, whether partial or complete) and 'circumnavigation' in his ongoing investigation into the disappearance of Harold Absalon, the Mayor's transport advisor, who remained missing presumed dead.

24

AND HE WONDERED about the other quadrants around what he had, intermittently, hitherto, been calling a headland, which is to say his right leg, even though, as previously stated, on at least one occasion, this was at odds, metaphorically speaking, which is to say that, as a metaphor or simile (whichever it was), it was at odds with the metaphor or simile (as before) of circumnavigation in the sense of his left foot circumnavigating the landmass, to call it that to be consistent with the initial metaphor, represented by his right leg as anchored to the ground by his right foot. Leaving aside, now, the idea that his right leg was anchored to the ground by his right foot since this would only serve to complicate matters further given that the anchor was a nautical rather than a terrestrial trope which was at odds with the idea he had developed and was trying to establish in his investigation into the disappearance of Harold Absalon, the Mayor's transport advisor, who was missing presumed dead, of the right leg and foot as being either a substantial landmass (in the scenario, this, in which the left foot simply passes around that headland) or the entire planet upon which he and we are, presumably, situated whilst apprehending, through whatever means ongoingly mysterious to Marguerite, his ongoing investigation (in the scenario in which the left foot circumnavigated, whether wholly or partially, that right leg and foot). Yet there was nothing, he now realised, as his left foot approached the albeit not very sharp crease that, as it were, ran down the front of his right-side trouser leg, to prevent him from referring to a whole or partial circumnavigation of a landmass – provided, of course, that landmass was an island, which is to say, provided, of course, that landmass was surrounded (and he didn't need to say 'on all sides') by water in the form of the ocean(s); in other words, just because the term circumnavigation had often been associated, particularly during a phase of history of epic seafaring and colonial conquest and war, with the phrase 'of the globe' this did not mean that he must use this coinage, so to speak; after all, strictly speaking, the term circumnavigation only implied the combination, and relationship between, two elements, despite the historical, colonial resonances: circularity (hence the need, on occasion, for the modifiers 'partial', 'complete' etc.) and wayfaring or -finding (or both); hence the term circumnavigation could quite properly be applied to said landmass, regardless of whether that landmass consisted of numerous nation states (in the case where, say, it had been defined, at a certain historical juncture, as a continent), a single nation state (where that landmass may more properly be referred to, perhaps, as an island), part of a nation state (in the case where the island was only a part of that nation state – where, say, that nation state had annexed it, as it might euphemistically be referred to, for its natural resources, its strategic location or due to its sheer proximity to the remainder of that nation state, for instance) or not part of a nation state (in the scenario where the concept of nation states had not emerged, or had not yet emerged for the landmass in question, or had emerged and then ceased as a concept for that landmass or in general) in that the juxtaposition of a landmass surrounded by one or more oceans (with the number of oceans surrounding the landmass presumably being dependent, in part, on the category of landmass: continental, archipelagogical, or whatever) was sufficient, strictly speaking, for someone (or some*thing*) to circumnavigate – or attempt, at least, to circumnavigate – whether wholly or partially, that landmass, implying that the phrase 'passing around a headland' was not, in fact, inconsistent, metaphorically speaking (which is to say that it was not at odds in terms of tropes, which is to say, tropically, although this adverbial use added further complications, which he refrained from exploring, as it were (etc.)) with the concept of circumnavigation, particularly if one took the headland of the landmass in question to be a protuberant section which, in the case of his left foot, he took to be the albeit not very sharp crease that as it were ran down the front of his right-side trouser leg and which that foot decisively now passed in its continued circumnavigation of that right leg and his continued investigation into the disappearance of Harold Absalon, the Mayor's transport advisor, who, as we know, had been, and, as far as we can tell, remains, missing presumed dead.

25

G IVEN THAT HIS left foot had, now, moved from the arc of the sector formed by the intersection of a circle of radius r, where r is equal to half the distance between the centre of the right foot and the nearest point on the longitudinal centreline of the occupied or unoccupied skateboard to his right, centred on the centre of his right foot, with the projection of a straight line from the centre of that circle through the seam running, as it were, down the left side of his right-side trouser leg and the projection forwards from that centre of a straight line through the crease running, as it were, down the front of that right-side trouser leg, to the arc of the sector formed by the intersection of that circle with the line projected forwards from its centre through the crease running, as it were, down the front of that right-side trouser leg and the projection, to the right, of a straight line from that centre through the seam running, as it were, down the right side of that right-side trouser leg, it may now be apparent, Marguerite thought, as that foot continued sketching the curve around what might also be referred to as the eastern half of the north-western quadrant of that partially revolved partial figure-of-eight (which is to say the quadrant formed by the projection of straight lines northwards and eastwards, respectively, from the centre of the right foot at right angles to each other through the crease running, as it were, down the front of his right-side trouser leg and the seam running, as it were, down the right side of same, such that that section of that partially revolved partial figure-of-eight intercepted those lines from that crease and that seam, thereby *ipso facto* demarcating that particular quadrant of that invisible partially revolved partial figure), with the revolution, to spell it out, as it were, for the first time, being a quarter turn either clockwise or anti-clockwise around its central point (taking the figure-of-eight to be symmetrical along both its axes), that his left foot, once it had traced the curves around the top-left and bottom-right, or north-west and south-east, respectively, quadrants of that partial figure-of-eight revolved, by a quarter turn, in either a clockwise or an anti-clockwise direction around its central axis, would not, in addition, trace that figure's remaining quadrant arc, namely the top-right, or north-eastern, one (with this arc lending itself to being described, of course, as the northern half of the circumference of a circle centred on a point equidistant from the central point of that partially revolved partial figure and the nearest point on the longitudinal centreline of the occupied or unoccupied skateboard to his right, with a radius equal to the distance between those points, which is to say, between the point equidistant from the central point of that partially revolved partial figure and the nearest point on the longitudinal centreline of the occupied or unoccupied skateboard to his right), given that the most easterly point of that figure would, more or less, correspond with the nearest point on the longitudinal centreline of the occupied or unoccupied skateboard immediately, or thereabouts, to his right, meaning that it was the destination and termination – at least of the route traced by that partial figure-of-eight revolved by a quarter turn, clockwise or anti-clockwise, around its axis, this being the reason why his left foot, once it had finished tracing the curves around the top-left and bottom-right, or north-west and south-east, respectively, quadrants of that partial figure-of-eight revolved, by a quarter turn, in either a clockwise or an anti-clockwise direction around its central axis, would not, in addition, trace that figure's remaining quadrant arc, namely the top-right, or north-eastern, one since, in short, the left foot would, at that point, Marguerite hoped, have landed upon the upward-facing surface of the occupied or unoccupied skateboard to his right, meaning that that foot would not need to continue its journey along that partially revolved partial figure, which, indeed, was why he had referred to it as a *partial* figure-of-eight in the first place – leaving aside, for now and maybe forever, the fact that not all typefaces represent the figure-of-eight as being symmetrical around the horizontal (and perhaps even the vertical) axis, which is to say, around the horizontal or vertical axes, meaning that *quadrant* arc was not the correct term and that radius r could not be taken to be *half* the distance between the centre of the right foot and the nearest point on the longitudinal centreline of the occupied or unoccupied skateboard to his right, and the fact that Marguerite's general direction in his ongoing investigation into the disappearance of Harold Absalon, the Mayor's transport advisor, who remained missing presumed dead, was actually easterly, rather than northerly, which is to say that the ramp down which he, the occupied or unoccupied skateboard, the erstwhile (or otherwise) skateboarder and, presumably, ourselves, continued to move; the ramp descending in the opposite direction towards the mouth of the pedestrian underpass proper; and the pedestrian underpass itself beneath that tree-lined avenue with a row of showrooms on one side of it and a vast expanse of parkland on the other, were, in fact, aligned in an east-west (or west-east[17]) rather than a north-south (or south-north) direction, whilst the horizontal rectangular plane, which was, he hoped, the area within which he would meet the woman in the tight-fitting pinstriped suit in advance of his pursuer was, conversely (given it was at right angles to the connecting approaches to that pedestrian underpass), aligned in a north-south (or south-north) rather than an east-west (or west-east) direction, meaning that the cardinal points referred to earlier should themselves be revolved through ninety degrees, for clarity, something Marguerite left those, such as ourselves, to do in their (/our) own time given the pressing nature of his investigation and the fact that his left foot had, in fact, now transitioned from clockwise to counter-clockwise radial rather than angular (note) rotation, meaning not only that it had moved through the centre of that partially revolved partial figure-of-eight, which is to say from the sectoral arc of radius r_1, in the scenario, now, in which the figure-of-eight is taken to be asymmetrical around its horizontal but not its vertical axis, where r_1 is equal to the distance between the centre of his right foot and the centre of that partially revolved partial figure-of-eight bounded by a left-right projection through the seams running, as it were, down both sides of his right-side trouser leg and centred on the centre of his right foot, to the sectoral arc of radius r_2, where r_2 is equal to the distance between a point equidistant from the centre of that partially revolved partial figure and the nearest point on the longitudinal centreline of that occupied or unoccupied skateboard

---

17 Eventually, though, we entered into a nightly routine of working and dining together in that underground vault. Still I was determined not to lay a finger on her, despite the evident chemistry between us.

to his right centred on that point and bounded by the same left-right projection, r_1 being greater than r_2 in the scenario where that figure had been revolved clockwise, by a quarter turn, around its central axis, or less than r_2 where it had been revolved *anti*-clockwise, by a quarter turn, around the same axis, but that it had embarked upon its final approach to the upward-facing surface of that occupied or unoccupied skateboard immediately, or thereabouts, to his right, with all that that entailed.

26

A ND THE FACT that his left foot had now passed
around the first part of the sectoral arc of radius r_2,
where r_2 is equal to the distance between a point equidistant from the centre of that partially revolved partial figure
and the nearest point on the longitudinal centreline of that
occupied or unoccupied skateboard to his right centred on
that point and bounded by a left-right projection through the
seams running, as it were, down both sides of his right-side
trouser leg must mean that it, which is to say his left foot,
was quite close, now, to the skateboard in question, and the
way in which he reasoned this was the fact that his left foot,
having passed around the first part of that sectoral arc whose
boundary condition and, Marguerite hoped, terminating position, as it were, was the nearest point on the longitudinal
centreline of that occupied or unoccupied skateboard to his
right, combined with the fact that the distance between the
centreline and the nearside edge of that still-moving skateboard to his right was also more-or-less equal in length to
radius r_2, which is to say, equal to the distance between a point
equidistant from the centre of that partially revolved partial
figure and the nearest point on the longitudinal centreline of
that occupied or unoccupied skateboard to his right centred
on that point, meant that his left foot should, in theory, be
approaching that nearside edge en route to the nearest point
on that longitudinal centreline. Why then, when he took in

the juxtaposition between foot and board in his increasingly blurred peripheral vision did he find that the still-moving skateboard remained resolutely still one radial length from that foot meaning that, once that foot had finished tracing the partially revolved partial figure-of-eight, it would land on that nearside edge rather than on the nearest point on the longitudinal centreline of that still-moving board? What he could not countenance at this stage of his investigation into the disappearance of Harold Absalon, the Mayor's transport advisor, who was missing presumed dead, was that this was a further misjudgement on his part, something that he took to be most uncharacteristic. Instead, he took this gulf still to be bridged as evidence that the skateboard was still occupied, that the occupant was, as feared, in the process of manoeuvring around him to the right so as to intercept the woman in the tight-fitting pinstriped suit who, he noticed, was staring intently into the small round metal case inside the briefcase, and that Marguerite must do everything in his power to get to her before them.

27

BOTH MARGUERITE AND the woman in the tight-fit-ting pinstriped suit would also, of course, be in motion and were also looking, he thought, to couple with one another as each continued their respective (and he hoped intersecting) trajectories towards the horizontal rectangular plane; further, he hoped, as before, that his initial, hopefully successful coupling operation with the skateboard prior to his coupling to or with the consensual woman in the tight-fitting pinstriped suit would, in fact, facilitate, if that was not too slippery a word, this latter coupling in that it would enable him to as it were shake off the skateboarder, regardless of whether they were riding or walking, whilst using their board to speed into the arms (or other fragrant appendages) of the aforementioned woman. What, though, were the differences, he wondered, as he noticed that the woman in the tight-fitting pinstriped suit was leaning towards the small round metal case within the briefcase as she applied lipstick to her lips[18], between the two types of coupling that he wished in short order to effect? He knew that in some instances, which is to say in some circum-stances surrounding the coupling between human beings and their self-propelled vehicles (of whatever wheel diameter) that

18 This was a delicate, intimate project we were engaged in – poring over reference materials together, examining records, scrutinising artefacts – and one whose success would not only bring down Knox and his dynasty but would bring a concomitant boost to myself in my own burgeoning political ambitions, whose starting point was, of course, much humbler.

there was, in fact, a mechanism that physically attached itself to that vehicle so as to facilitate, which is to say to make easier, that very self-propulsion; and what he had in mind here was what he thought was known as the toe clip on certain types of pedal, this latter being the main contact point between the foot (or, more specifically in the case of the clip, the toe or toes) and that specific non-motorised vehicle (and, indeed, it could plausibly be asserted that this contact point was the main means of transferring that very propulsive force from the person in question to the non-motorised vehicle as the means of transporting it and oneself). In the case of the toe clip, then, what took place, so far as he could tell, was that the clip was inserted somehow into the pedal, the foot, or feet, having prior to this been inserted into the bespoke shoe or shoes that contained that clip or those clips (and perhaps, for our sake, he would, for now, simply limit himself to the singular, something that, in any case, would, he thought, strengthen the case that he was trying to make about the similarities and differences between coupling with a self-propelled non-motor-ised vehicle of whatever wheel diameter and with an attractive (wo)man (or, granted, someone who is transgender) regardless, really, of the tightness or otherwise of their clothing), and it was this very means of attachment (a word that he would, no doubt, return to) that was, in fact, one of the similarities, in the case of the pedal bike within the sub-category that he was alluding to, with the situation in which one coupled (as a man, note), with an attractive (or otherwise) man, woman or, simply, person, a situation, remember, that Marguerite wished to speedily but not hastily bring about with respect to the woman in the tight-fitting pinstriped suit. Marguerite decided to spell it out for those of a less subtle or, granted, less sexually experienced disposition, as his foot, the left, approached the nearside edge of the upward-facing surface of the still-moving skateboard with the intention of both mounting that board and dislodging any occupant: the clip resembled the male and its housing the female sexual organ, and it was this similarity that he had been drawing out in his inquiry into the differences and similarities between self to non-motorised vehicle and inter-personal coupling, and he hoped, at this stage, that it would be taken as read that even if the persons involved in the interpersonal coupling did not actually fit into the characterisation of male and female respectively that, in the build up to, during, and at what was traditionally referred to as the climax (in the case where there was one, or more) within that specific coupling, they would, at least, assume those roles at least for the duration of that particular encounter, or part thereof; in other words even if the one doing the penetration was not male, or, at least, did not feel comfortable, in the moments preceding the moment of coupling (if not the moment of climax) in identifying themselves in that way then, for the sake of clarity in the exposition of Marguerite's position, he (referring to Marguerite – don't worry) would still refer to that protagonist, to call them that, as 'male', with the consensual as it were recipient of this penetrative organ/device being momentarily defined in Marguerite's system as 'female', again regardless of whether the latter felt comfortable in assuming that mantle outside of that specific encounter, or part thereof. He was, then, simply talking about roles, rather than anything fixed, in the foregoing comparison, with the person (to retain the singular, no doubt to the relief of the more prudish amongst us) engaged in the more penetrative aspect of that particular encounter, or part thereof, as 'the male' (regardless of whether ordinarily they would define themselves as female, male, both, or neither); similarly (but conversely) the person who was, or would be, as it were on the receiving end of that penetration Marguerite would momentarily, for clarity, define as 'female' (regardless, as before, of whether they would define themselves in that way under different, or indeed similar, circumstances). This, then, was one similarity, in the case of the toe clip attached to the pedal of a push bike (a term Marguerite had to fervently refrain from getting started on, fearing that it would divert him further from the main body of his investigation): that of the insertion of a 'male' member into a receptive 'female' housing (and note, that this member may, in fact, for instance, be a rechargeable device employed by one comfortably self-defined female on another; or of one male on another; or of one female on a male; or of one who would not wish to identify as male or female, on another who similarly avoided such neat categorisation; or of a male on a female; or of a transgender person on a male; or of a female on a transgender person; or of a male on a transgender person; or of a transgender person on a female; or, to recapitulate by way only of pronouns, of: she on him; he on her; he on him; she on her; he on them; they on him; she on them; and they on her, with the non-gender-specific pronouns taken to refer to the transgender individual in the singular, rather than male, female and/or transgender persons in the plural). But that was not the case, was it, in Marguerite's situation, as he placed the three smallest toes of his left foot upon the skateboard, which listed badly to the left? There was neither toe-clip nor housing, so far as he could tell, which is to say that he was, he presumed, wearing his trusty (but, by now, not very fragrant) old boots, whilst the surface of the skateboard was, presumably, more or less flat, and did not contain any perturbations that could, even with the most febrile imagination, be defined as male or female. Marguerite hoped, as he realised, given the amount the board had tilted to the left, that it was, in fact unoccupied (aside, that is, from the three toes of his left foot that he had placed, precariously, upon it), that this did not portend a similar non-penetrative and perhaps even asexual encounter with the woman in the tight-fitting pinstriped suit given that he had an increasing urge, he realised, evidenced by the concomitant bodily changes, to go all the way with her, as it's known, in furtherance, he felt sure, of his investigation into the disappearance of Harold Absalon, the Mayor's transport advisor, who was missing presumed dead.

28

AND ALMOST IMMEDIATELY he was at the point of losing control, having coupled precariously with the skateboard, although, note, that this was a different category of losing control to that which occurred with the other form of coupling, which is to say, the coupling with a sexual partner of whatever complexion of gender, with the former type of loss of control being a consequence, in Marguerite's case, of the fact that, whilst the three smallest toes of his left foot had been attaining the upwards facing surface of the skateboard that had, until that moment, he now realised, been freewheeling under its own steam, as it were, down the decline towards the horizontal rectangular landing plane of both that decline and the stairs down which the woman in the tight-fitting pinstriped suit would, he hoped, imminently descend, and which now, presumably, continued travelling down that decline under the propulsive force of those three (and counting) of Marguerite's toes, his right foot, which remained in contact, still, with that decline, had been adopting a not dissimilar position in that only the three smallest toes of that right foot now remained in contact with that downward-sloping surface, although in the case of the right foot this was a precursor to that foot (and those toes) losing contact with that surface en route to its (and their) journey around the left leg/foot, in a counter-clockwise direction this time, prior to coupling, in turn, with the upward-facing surface of the skateboard spatially in advance, Marguerite thought, of its counterpart the left foot, with its toes. It was, then, a consequence of this precarious juxtaposition of contact and movement that, in coupling with the board thus during its, and his, onward journey down the slope, Marguerite had asserted that he felt he was on the brink of losing control, in that, given the tenuous connection, through what had been the three smallest toes of his right foot but which now, given the elapsed time since submitting that particular report, pertained only to the *two* smallest toes of that foot with the slope leading down to the horizontal rectangular landing plane (etc.), and the similar tenuous connection between the left foot and its toes (and in the latter case it was only the big toe, now, which was *not* in contact with the moving upward-facing surface of the skateboard (although note that, in Marguerite's case, the toe adjacent to that big toe, which we can infer had just touched down, as it were, upon that surface, was, for the record, larger, in fact – lengthwise – than the so-called big toe, and it was for this reason that he thought of it as the 'bigger' or 'biggest' toe, depending upon his mood on the day that he was thinking about it)), it was possible that he might actually fall down, which, aside from being unprofessional, undignified, and, in drawing attention to himself, might adversely affect his investigation into the disappearance of Harold Absalon, the Mayor's transport advisor, who was missing presumed dead, might also scupper his plan to both couple and lose control (in the latter sense) with the woman in the tight-fitting pinstriped suit who he hoped rapidly to approach in due course. Given the fact, though, that the bigger or biggest (depending) toe of his left foot had, in fact, now attained the upward-facing surface of the moving skateboard, thereby affording more stability through that connection than had hitherto been the case, with this toe presumably being followed (and Marguerite refrained, at this moment, from using the phrase 'hot on the heels', for what he hoped were obvious reasons) in short order by the so-called big toe of that foot, could it still be said, in any case, that he was at risk of losing control (in the former sense)? He thought that it could given that, in placing four (and counting) toes of his left foot upon the upward-facing surface of that latterly vacant skateboard, he found that surface to be inclining towards him, which is to say that the board had started leaning, or listing, to the left in the way that it was designed to do through some combination, presumably, of mechanical articulation via the wheels to enable one to steer as one propelled oneself through this means. It was, then, the combination of placing more of his weight (and of the toes of his left foot) upon that board whilst retaining less of his weight (and of the toes of his right foot) upon the relatively stable ground provided by the slope leading down to the aforementioned horizontal rectangular plane that had resulted in the latterly vacant skateboard listing badly to the left which, in turn, had resulted in him asserting that he remained, as far as he could tell, at the point, still, of losing control (in the former sense) which, as before, would reduce his chances, he thought, of losing control (in the latter sense) with the woman in the tight-fitting pinstriped suit following their abrupt, consensual coupling. And the difference between the two senses related, perhaps, to the added emotional and biological dimension to the latter whilst one of the similarities related, quite simply, to the shared use of the concept of falling, Marguerite thought, as he realised that he had, in fact, fallen in love with the woman in the tight-fitting pinstriped suit many years previously[19].

19 I sensed that Hazel was aware of the power shifting, on a knife edge, towards me, her allegiances changing accordingly.

29

WITH HIS RIGHT foot having momentarily become airborne – and the leftwards tilt of the skateboard having become ever more pronounced – he found that, rather than circling around the left leg, in a counter-clockwise direction, as had been anticipated previously by him, such that it would land in advance, spatially, of its counterpart (to use that nomenclature for his left foot, for the sake of brevity) on the upward-facing surface of the board, his right foot had, in fact, immediately returned to ground, as it were, although it was a portion of ground (or, more specifically, of the slope leading down to the aforementioned horizontally aligned rectangular landing place) in advance, spatially, of that from which it had taken off, given that, in the interim, his weight had momentarily (with this moment *ipso facto* being precisely contemporaneous with the flight of his right foot, hence the deliberate repeated use of the word 'momentarily') been fully supported, through the toes and ball, now, of his left foot, on the still-moving skateboard, by that skateboard. In other words, given that the skateboard had continued to move whilst his weight was, momentarily (as before) fully supported upon and by it, with the duration of this momentary support being delimited firstly by the instant at which his right foot had taken off, as it's known, from the downward slope – and, more specifically, by the instant at which the little toe of his right foot had taken off, as it's known, from the downward slope (a toe, note, that in Marguerite's case was, indeed, the smallest in that collection, which is to say that the little toe of his right foot was the littlest toe, in both girth and length, of that foot and that the little toe of his left foot was the littlest toe, in both girth and length, of *that* foot, although he had never had a chance to compare these two small toes to see which, in fact, was the smallest of the two), and lastly by the instant at which that foot – and toe – had landed again upon that slope, it was inevitable, to his mind, that that foot would land (given the further condition of the skateboard not being stationary, and moving down, rather than up, that downwardly-, or granted, upwardly- (depending upon one's view- or vantage point) inclined slope) further down that slope than the position from which that foot – and that toe (which we can confidently say was – and perhaps still is – the smallest toe on that foot, if not on that body as a whole) – had embarked upon this momentary (etc.) airborne excursion.

What had prevented his right foot from accompanying his left, having performed an anti-clockwise circumnavigation of his left leg, upon the upward-facing surface of the leftward-leaning skateboard so as to facilitate his rapid coupling and concomitant loss of control with the woman in the tight-fitting pinstriped suit, he wondered, as he noticed that the woman in question had retrieved from the briefcase a crumpled fedora hat belonging, Marguerite thought, to Harold Absalon – the first clear lead in Marguerite's investigation to date? Was it the very fact of this leftwards tilt that had resulted in the potentially epic partial circumnavigation being aborted before it had hardly even started? In other words, had the increasingly pronounced leftwards tilt of the surface of the board, implying as it did a counter-clockwise rotation of that board around its long central axis (when viewed, note, from the rear of the board), somehow prevented the counter-clockwise partial circumnavigation of his right foot around his left leg, a partial circumnavigation whose ultimate purpose was to place the right foot upon that board in advance, spatially, of the related left foot (with this relation being anything but tenuous, given that it consisted of a direct connection with that left leg in the form of bone, sinews etc.) somewhere, presumably, just on the other side of that long central axis so as to as it were right the ship, which is to say, so as to prevent the board from as it were completely capsizing (to continue, for now, the nautical metaphor)? Was it the case, though, that that counter-clockwise rotation around the long central axis of the skateboard (when viewed from the rear of the board) had, in fact, advanced further than he had anticipated such that, by the time the right foot had taken off from the downwardly- (etc.) inclined surface, the whole arrangement had become unstable and untenable to the extent that he had no choice but to return that right foot, almost immediately, to (a slightly different portion of) earth, with the implication being that the left foot must also as it were retrace its footsteps in reversing its position from being upon the listing skateboard to being upon the ground once more, with no guarantee, given the continued movement of the skateboard based on the momentum it had already acquired, of revisiting and successfully accomplishing this partial, revolved figure-of-eight movement with his feet as a means of placing them upon that moving board as an aid to coupling – and losing control – with the woman in the tight-fitting pinstriped suit, all, of course, in the service of his investigation into the disappearance of Harold Absalon, the Mayor's transport advisor, who, as far as we can tell, remained missing presumed dead? Would the left foot, in other words, now reverse its previous manoeuvre (assuming, given the reversal of the right foot that the left would not remain on the upward-facing surface of the still-moving skateboard), which is to say would the left foot now circumnavigate the right leg en route to a position further up, and to the right of that right foot, upon that decline? Marguerite thought this highly unlikely given the progress of the skateboard, and the left foot upon it, down that slope towards the woman in the tight-fitting pinstriped suit, who was, at that moment, in the process of placing the fedora on her head. In other words, and to recap, his right foot had initially been spatially both in advance and to the left of his left foot on that decline – this as a means of using the remainder of his body to block the progress of the skateboarder behind him (before Marguerite had himself momentarily boarded the subsequently vacated skateboard); his left foot had then epically circumnavigated his right leg, tracing, as it did so, a partial, inverted figure-of-eight such that it alighted upon (or perhaps, as before, boarded) that vacant skateboard, meaning that that left foot was, following this boarding (in two senses of the term now), both spatially in advance and to the right of (and, indeed, above) his right foot, which had, of course, initially remained upon the decline leading down to the horizontal rectangular plane upon which both he and the woman in the tight-fitting pinstriped suit (and, presumably, the skateboarder, whether skateboarding or otherwise) would, he hoped, subsequently land, couple and lose control (except, of course, the latter, which is to say, the skateboarder whom, Marguerite clearly wanted to stay out of it), whether they remained upright or modelled the horizontal nature of that surface by lying down, together, upon it; and his right foot had, then, taken off, as it were, as the skateboard listed alarmingly to the left due to the pressure of the left foot which had been placed to the left of the axis formed by the longitudinal centreline of that board, such that the right foot had abruptly landed again, albeit further down the slope towards the mutual landing, coupling and control-losing horizontal rectangular plane that formed the interface between an as it were forward-facing slope leading down to it and a rearward-facing (from Marguerite's, and presumably, for that reason, from our own point of view) leading away from it and towards what is known as the mouth, for perhaps obvious reasons, of the pedestrian underpass which crossed the broad, tree-lined avenue on the other side of which lay both the vast expanse of parkland and, one hoped, the solution to the various conundra that Marguerite, and we, have been set in the foregoing (including, of course, within previous volumes). The question, then, given the foregoing was, to repeat, whether the left foot, in alighting from the still-moving skateboard such that it (that foot and that board) was now spatially in advance of the as it were grounded right foot (although, as before, note that this left foot was, in fact, at a more advanced, which is to say higher, elevation than the right foot given its continued, albeit precarious, attainment of the upper surface of the skateboard, a surface raised, as it was, above that decline by a height in exceedance, of course, of the aforementioned wheels) would repeat its circumnavigation of the right leg such that it would return to a position that was, relatively speaking (that is, in relation to the relative position of the feet), the same as that from which it had embarked upon this epic journey, which is to say a position above, and to the right of that right foot, with both feet, as before, upon the surface of the slope again. He thought it highly unlikely. After all, he had accomplished, he thought, what he had set out to do within this branch of his inquiry, which was to prevent the erstwhile skateboarder from reaching the woman in the tight-fitting pinstriped suit before Marguerite himself had done so, thereby preventing this pursuer from coupling with that woman, regardless of whether this coupling was accompanied by any loss of control on the part of the so-called male or female protagonists to this coupling or, in the case where either or both did not accept that gender identity or those gender identities, simply the perpetrator and recipient, as it were, respectively, of the consensual penetrative act of a sexual nature that both would engage in, assuming for now, that both parties would not engage in both penetrative perpetration and reception, as it were, at the same time, which would only serve to blur the boundaries further, to Marguerite's mind. No, the way now lay clear for him to that woman, meaning, quite simply, that he could place both feet upon that decline in their more natural positions, which is to say, he could place his left foot, once it left the surface of the upward-facing surface of the still-moving skateboard, to the left of, in advance of, and below, his right foot, as a precursor to moving that right foot, subsequently, to a position to the right of, in front of, and below, the left foot[20], without any assistance from any vehicle, regardless of whether that vehicle was self-propelled, small-wheeled, or whatever.

20 The heightened tension that now existed between us led me to presume she was leading me, on that final occasion together, to one of the many isolated study areas within the archive as a place of last resort for the assignation I felt had been approaching for some time and whose inevitability I now accepted given all that we'd been through together.

30

H E HAD BEEN hoping, he realised, for what some
might term a negotiated separation, which is to say
between his left foot and the upward-facing surface of the
skateboard upon which it continued to be connected via its
ball and toes, rather than the precipitous violent separation
between the two parties, so called, that he feared might now
occur, as he noticed that the woman in the tight-fitting pinstriped suit had closed – and presumably locked – the briefcase and had removed it from the position it had occupied
upon her angled right thigh. And in a negotiated separation
– and some might call it a divorce, even though this term only
really applied to domestic arrangements, which is to say that
it related to arrangements pertaining to home rather than
to locations distant from same – there would, as the name
implied, be a discussion about its terms, which is to say a
discussion, albeit sometimes heated (but not ordinarily violent,
he thought, in this scenario), about how the separation might
take place, as had been the case between Isobel and Harold
Absalon shortly before the latter's disappearance.

Granted the term could also be applied in the international
arena, even though internationality immediately implied the
non-domestic. And the way in which it was applied in that
latter arena, which is to say in an international setting, related,
Marguerite thought, to situations in which there had been a
pre-existing partnership, such as a trade or other agreement

(based, inevitably, on shared views and values – a shared sense of 'home' even – for some, at least, of the inhabitants – the 'subjects' – of the nation- or city-states concerned) either entered into freely – and perhaps even democratically – or imposed, historically or more latterly, by force, with the implication, in the latter scenario, which is to say, to extend the metaphor further, that of forced marriage, whether longstanding or more recent, of a reduced likelihood of a negotiated (which is to say non-violent) separation, although, even in the latter scenario, this, which is to say a negotiated separation, may be possible, with (or because of) sufficient water having passed under the bridge, as it were, which is to say sufficient historical distance between the acts of conquest, subjugation, colonisation and imposed government, and the present day, which is to say the day, say, of commencement of the so-called divorce proceedings, such that later generations of conquered and colonised (etc.) subjects might even, now, identify sufficiently with their forebears' former colonisers (and vice versa, which is to say that the forebears of those former colonisers might identify sufficiently, by now, with the forebears of the former conquered and colonised subjects) to the extent that, where they do seek a separation, that that separation is a negotiated rather than a violent one (with the distinction between the two being, of course, dependent, in part, upon the identification between forebears of former colonised (etc.) and coloniser (etc.) being sufficiently strong for an ongoing kinship to prevail but insufficiently strong to want to continue to live under the same roof, to extend the domestic metaphor still further, whilst, granted, introducing *ipso facto* something unsettlingly incestual into the proceedings).

In the case, though, of an agreement (relating to trade,

regulation and/or the free movement of subjects, say) that had been freely entered into by the governments (or, granted, monarchs[21]/heads of state) involved, even if not every one of the subjects of those respective governments or monarchies had agreed to the terms – or fact, which is to say the existence – of that original agreement, and of subsequent amendments and additions to it, then the prospect of a negotiated, which is to say a non-violent, separation – 'divorce' as we are metaphorically referring to it here, even though this term strictly speaking should only really be applied in a domestic setting – should be much much higher than in a scenario in which the agreement had not, in fact, been entered into freely by both (or, where there are more than two, which is to say in situations of non-bipartite agreements, all) of the parties concerned (as described above – not that Marguerite can have any real sense of what this 'above' might refer to). And this is not even to go into the disastrous (for one, both, or all parties) scenario of a non-negotiated non-violent separation, which is to say the scenario of a separation between parties who have failed to reach any sort of agreement, perhaps despite their best efforts, as it is known, or because one or more party/ parties to the agreement and partnership (or members thereof, which is to say members of the parties to that agreement and partnership, regardless of whether those members were directly involved in the negotiations concerned, were in a position to influence those involved in those negotiations, both, or neither) wanted that outcome, which is to say, wanted to exit (as it has also come to be known in some circumstances amongst some people) the agreement without reaching an

21 There was nothing to suggest I was wrong in my assumption as we approached a door in the basement that I'd never previously encountered.

agreement on how that exit should occur – this for doctrinal purposes, which is to say based on views and values that could, in some circumstances, be taken to be antithetical to the inspiration behind the original agreement and to which the original agreement may have been based (even if, over time, the views and values enshrined, as it would be known, in the original agreement – and even in subsequent amendments and additions to it – may have degenerated and/or been eroded).

And what Marguerite realised, as he noticed that the woman in the tight-fitting pinstriped suit had removed her right foot from its position upon the dwarf wall that formed the base of the railings to the right of the steps leading down to the horizontal rectangular plane that also provided the landing position for the ramp down which Marguerite continued to move, was that he – which is to say, more specifically, his left foot – was heading either for a disastrous or for a violent (or both) separation from the board in question, and the reason that this realisation had dawned upon him (this being what realisations do, implying, as in the scenario of the rising sun – which is, of course (to be explicit) the original reference point – a slow enlightening, albeit, in Marguerite's case, a chilling one, with this latter point being, of course, contrary, metaphorically speaking, to the original source), was based on the fact that, all along, it had, that foot, been involved in what he now took to be a forced marriage with that board in that the latter had never been his, or its, to possess (not, he hastened to add, that he thought that a spouse could – or should – ever be thought of as a possession) given that it belonged, presumably, to the erstwhile skateboarder meaning that Marguerite had taken it against its (which is to say, against its owner's) will, with the likely, if not inevitable, outcome of (as before) a disastrous and/or violent separation from it – this is in the case where no agreement to that separation is reached prior to the separation taking place, although he didn't know, now, what an agreement might mean in the immediate case in question – that of a left foot as it were perching, precariously, close to the edge of the upward-facing surface of a skateboard that until that moment of contact between foot and board could, only in retrospect, be taken to have been freewheeling unoccupied down the inclined surface leading to the horizontal rectangular plane of the approach, as it might be called, to that pedestrian underpass that was so central to his investigation into the disappearance of Harold Absalon, the Mayor's transport advisor, who had been, and, we think, remains, missing and is presumed dead.

31

HOW LONG WOULD his left foot retain its precarious perch on the back of that skateboard, he wondered, as he noticed that the left foot of the woman in the tight-fitting pinstriped suit was now placed right at the edge of the top step of the flight leading down to the horizontal rectangular plane that also formed the landing position of the ramp down which Marguerite continued to descend in the manner described? Before answering that question he felt a need to explore further how it had come to pass that he had started referring to what he had hitherto called the upward-facing surface of the skateboard as the back of same. Was it, he wondered, in reference to the horse, ass, donkey, mule and other beast of burden such as the ox (or was oxen the plural of same?) that he had made this connection? After all, it was upon the back of such beasts that one momentarily resided in the situation where one was using them to convey oneself (as in the current instance) rather than using these beasts of burden to convey goods (as in the aforementioned cases of the wheeled suitcase, parcel trolley and the like). Was it, then, through some atavistic echo of this earlier period in the evolution of human conveyance that he had slipped, momentarily or ongoingly, into referring to the more or less upward-facing surface of the skateboard upon which his left foot continued, for now, precariously to reside, as the back of that board? After all, would it not make more sense to refer to the area of that board to the rear of that left foot as the back of that skateboard, whilst, concomitantly referring to the section forward of that foot as the front of same? Were he to turn around to address the erstwhile skateboarder behind him – the owner, Marguerite assumed, of the board that his left foot continued to perch precariously upon; and were he, during that address, to ask that erstwhile skateboarder – and continued skateboard-owner – to point to the back of his own skateboard would he not point to that portion behind Marguerite's left foot? Could it not be contended that this pointing would, in fact, be ambiguous, taking in, as it would, both the upward-facing surface and the rear-most portion of the same still-moving board? And given this ambiguous response, would it not be best for us, with Marguerite's assistance, to settle this issue for ourselves, Marguerite wondered, as, whilst steadying himself with the use of an increasingly outstretched left arm, his left foot finally left the back of the skateboard in question, assuming that, in continuing to refer to that part of the skateboard in that way, whilst the meaning is still unresolved, that it is at least sufficiently clear for us to understand what had just as it were occurred to Marguerite in his ongoing investigation into the disappearance of Harold Absalon, the Mayor's transport advisor, who was missing presumed dead? His left foot had, then, left the back of the skateboard in the same way as the left foot of a circus performer who had been standing on the back of their beplumed steed during a performance within, or a rehearsal for, what's known, for some reason, as the big top (and he hoped not to get sucked into exploring the differences and similarities between this still to be defined 'top', in the sense of the highest external part of a structure or other type of object and the 'back' which, in the case of the skateboard that was now free-wheeling unoccupied, once again, down the ramp leading to the horizontal rectangular plane that was also the landing area for the steps leading down to it from the right, which the woman in the tight-fitting pinstriped suit was now seemingly on the verge of descending, could also be taken as the highest and most exposed part, and which was, perhaps, in the process of being adequately defined) before jumping from the back of that steed into the sawdust of that extensive circular arena. It was, then, quite simply, Marguerite thought, the ubiquity of the horse, ass, donkey or mule in days of yore, as the primary – perhaps the only – non-human means of conveyance which meant that in our own age (or, at least, in the age in which Marguerite resided which might not, of course be the same age that we ourselves are now living through, although there was a presumptuousness on Marguerite's part that his investigation was sufficiently seminal to live on, through whatever means ongoingly mysterious to him, into another age, or other ages) we continued to refer to the upward-facing portion of our more modern conveyances, such as (and perhaps, in fact, limited to) the skate-, boogie-, snow- or surfboard, as the back, in the way that Marguerite had so recently done. And it was for reasons of this continued shared history, and for reasons of conciseness (something towards which he continually, and conscientiously, strived), that he would continue to refer to that part of the board as the back should he need, during the remainder of his inquiry, to refer to that section of that board, which was unlikely given the fact that his left foot was no longer located in that position but was, instead, now, as it were, airborne, en route not, as we know, to the position it had occupied on the down-slope before moving through its elaborate yet, to Marguerite's mind, elegant trajectory onto that board, but, instead, through force of gravity, to the aforementioned position to the right of, and below, the right foot on that slope leading down to the woman in the tight-fitting pinstriped suit and the rapidly, now, arriving culmination, we hope, of this convoluted and, to some, inconsequential inquiry.

32

IN FACT, IT was his right foot that must, now, complete the partial circumnavigation of the left leg in moving back towards its rightful place to the right of that left leg, although the figure that this partial circumnavigation would trace would, of necessity, Marguerite thought, be different to that traced previously by the left foot in circumnavigating the right leg as a means of attaining the back, as he had taken to calling it, of that still-moving skateboard, which was now on its way, uncontrolled, he thought, by human contact of any sort, towards the sheer, which is to say, the vertical, face of the wall on the other side of the horizontal rectangular landing plane towards which he, the woman in the tight-fitting pinstriped suit, the owner of the skateboard and all of us (if we make it that far) are all headed, as it's known. Why he wondered, did he think that it was the right rather than the left foot that must complete this partial circumnavigation even though it was, in fact (as we know, if we can recall), the left foot that was, still, airborne, having as it were decoupled itself from the back of that beast-of-the-modern-era (and this brought to mind the bronco, an avenue of inquiry that he declined to follow up at that moment and perhaps indefinitely)? In other words, why was he already anticipating the right foot's partial circumnavigation of the left leg when it was, in fact (if we continue to recall), the left foot that was, in fact, airborne, having as it were decoupled itself from the upward-facing surface of the skateboard, to return, perhaps just momentarily, to that nomenclature, meaning that it could, which is to say the left foot could, presumably, immediately commence its partial circumnavigation of the right leg en route to its as it were rightful place to the left of that right leg? Was it, he wondered, to do with this very use of the word 'rightful'? In other words, did his premature (to some) bringing into play of his right foot, in terms of its potentially imminent partial circumnavigation of his left leg as a means of attaining its as it were rightful place to the right of that left leg relate primarily to this very use of the term 'rightful', hinting, as it did (rather elegantly, to Marguerite's mind), to the fact that, once it had attained its as it were rightful place, it would be to the right of that left leg, thereby playing on at least two senses of the word 'right' which, were the left foot (which, remember, was the foot that had been – and continued, note, to be – airborne) to complete its partial circumnavigation of the *right* leg, could not be employed (given that – to make it explicit, for those who need further explication – the rightful place for the left leg was, in fact, to the *left* of the right leg)? Pleasing though he found all of this, and notwithstanding that he also thought this pleasure to be a compelling reason in itself for prematurely (to some) bringing the right foot into play whilst the left foot was still as it were airborne, it was not, in fact, the reason that he had brought that right foot into play. What, then, was the reason that he had brought the right foot into play, despite the fact that that right foot continued to remain firmly planted on the ground sloping down toward that horizontal rectangular plane towards which anyone who is anyone[22] is headed? The reason,

22 Nothing could have prepared me for what I found on entering that cold, dimly lit space, however, the door closing quietly behind me.

in short, that he had brought that right foot into play despite the fact that it continued to remain firmly planted in the aforementioned way was the relatively uncontrolled manner in which the left foot had been ejected, bronco-like (which is to say, like the unsaddled rider of an untrained, or partially trained, horse), from the back of that beast-of-the-modern era (and perhaps the equivalent creature for the surfboard was, in fact, the dolphin, given that these creatures, which were universally admired, did, he thought, allow people to ride them, which is to say to sit on their backs as they (the dolphins) swam, at least whilst in captivity); in other words, had his left foot decoupled itself from the skateboard in a more controlled fashion then it might have had an as it were partial reverse-circumnavigation of the right leg within its gift; but, given that it was, in fact, ejected in a somewhat unruly fashion, as previously adumbrated, and given that Marguerite had been in the process of placing what's known as his centre of gravity directly above the skateboard, this aforementioned force was acting upon that left foot without any counter-vailing one, which meant that that foot was moving more or less directly towards the ground, something that Marguerite had little choice about, even though it pained him to say it (which is to say that it added to the acute bodily pain he was already experiencing), given the conscientiousness with which he planned his investigations so as, in fact, to stay in control. It was, then, in ceding the control – at least in relation to the effects of the gravitational force acting upon his left foot – to which he was ordinarily accustomed to retaining that he had brought his right foot to mind, and had asserted that it was, in fact, this right foot that would embark upon a less epic partial circumnavigation of his left leg as a means of attaining its rightful place to the right of that left leg (and foot), and the reason he thought this partial circumnavigation by his right foot of his left leg would be less epic than the circumnavigation that his left foot had completed of his right leg was that, in finding its rightful place to the right of that left foot, the right foot would have to undergo a less circuitous route than the left foot had undergone in completing its circumnavigation: whereas the left foot had completed what came to be referred in the record books as a partially revolved partial figure-of-eight, the right foot would, quite simply, complete, if that's the word, a partial circumnavigation of the left leg in attaining its rightful (in more ways than one) place to the right of that left leg, something that it would now embark upon given that the left foot, having completed its unruly flight from the skateboard, had come to ground with a thud.

33

T HE RIGHT FOOT could not have commenced its partial circumnavigation of the left leg until this moment, which is to say until the left foot had fully returned to ground, even though, in certain circumstances, both feet could, of course, be airborne, as it's known, at the same time. In the case of running, for instance, both feet would be airborne, as it's known, at the same time, although not, of course, continually, otherwise that activity might be referred to as gliding or hovering; no, each foot, in turn, would be in contact with the ground in the case of running yet there would be an interlude between each contact during which both feet would, in fact, be airborne, and it was to this he had referred when he had asserted, at the commencement, or thereabouts, of this portion, to call it that, of his investigation, that, in the case of running, both feet would, in fact, be airborne at the same time, although with the aforementioned caveat of this not being continuous, which is to say that the feet would not continuously be airborne, otherwise this activity, instead of being referred to as running would, instead, be referred to as gliding or hovering, were this activity actually to be possible, which he didn't believe it was. Now in the case of walking, an activity that he was, once again, on the verge of engaging in having momentarily been at least on the brink of being propelled ongoingly forwards by means of a small-wheeled rider-propelled non-motorised vehicle in the form of a skateboard such that he would have intercepted the woman in the tight-fitting pinstriped suit before his pursuer, something that was now decidedly in jeopardy, it was imperative that one of the two feet (in the central case of bipeds to which he is tacitly referring here) be in contact with the ground at all times. It would not do, note, for both of the feet to be continually in contact with the ground throughout (which is why he had been so precise in stating that it must be one, rather than, say, *at least* one) since this would imply a different propulsive strategy, such as sliding or (in a different, more poetic sense now) gliding, rather than the requisite walking towards which everything in this branch of his investigation seems to be gravitating, just as his left foot had gravitated to ground to enable him to start positioning his right foot, through its partial circumnavigation of his left leg, to facilitate his continued perambulation in the manner described. No, it must be only one of the two feet in this central case of bipedal perambulation to which he was referring that must remain as it were grounded throughout. At the same time, though, it would not do simply to keep the *same* foot grounded throughout, since this would imply a profound stasis that would not be consistent with the speed and drama for which investigations that Marguerite was involved in were associated. Were he, for instance, as the ball of his right foot left the decline, to refuse to fully remove that right foot from that decline whilst allowing his left foot to roam as freely as it desired in a mistaken application of the rule that, when walking, one must keep one foot attached, as it were, to the sidewalk or other surface, then this attitude would not get him very far in his investigation into the disappearance of Harold Absalon, the Mayor's transport advisor, who was missing presumed dead. No, as may be apparent to the more astute amongst us, it was not that one could decide just to keep the one foot in contact with the ground; the feet must alternative in attaining the airborne state, just as in the case of running, whilst, unlike in the case of running, ensuring that one of them, the left or the right, remained in contact with the ground, and this, of course, was how the Olympic speed-walking was judged and, if necessary, penalised in the case where both feet left the ground at the same time.

Why though, Marguerite wondered, as the largest and smallest toes of his right foot became airborne, leaving just the middle three toes of that foot in contact with the decline, had he asserted that his right foot could not commence its partial circumnavigation of his left leg before the left foot had returned to ground? After all, there was no rule, as far as he could tell, when speed was of the essence, as it is known, that prevented both of his feet from being airborne at the same time. What was it then, if there was nothing in principle, that had prevented his right foot from commencing its partial circumnavigation of the left leg whilst the left foot was still airborne? Did it relate, he wondered, as these middle three toes of his right foot became airborne, meaning that the whole of that foot, now, was airborne, simply, as before, to the juxtaposition of his centre of gravity in relation to those feet? Had his centre of gravity been in advance of, rather than directly above, his left foot at the moment of its ejection from the back, as he continued to refer to it, of the skateboard then might he have been in a position, both literally and metaphorically, to launch his right foot such that it would as it were join his left foot in being airborne, which would have meant that he would not have had to wait for the left foot to return to ground, with or without a thud, before launching his right foot in the manner described?

Had his centre of gravity been more advanced, which is to say, had he built up more momentum in his mounting, or potential mounting, of the skateboard (to continue the equine imagery) then would it have been feasible, in other words, if not positively desirable, for him to launch his right foot into the air as this left foot continued to descend to ground, thereby saving him valuable time in his ongoing investigation? Or did this grounding of his right foot relate, in fact, to him not having injected sufficient force from this foot at the moment when his other foot (the left) was about to attain the back of the skateboard, meaning that there was insufficient momentum available to launch his right foot once the left had been ejected from that surface? Did it relate, as before, he wondered, to the abrupt nature of the ejection of that left foot, meaning that he had been unable to use the back of the skateboard, as he continued to refer to it, as a bulwark against which to apply sufficient force to launch the right foot in turn? It was, he thought, as the right foot of the woman in the tight-fitting pinstriped suit passed her left foot en route, finally, to the first step down the flight of steps leading down to the horizontal rectangular plane that also intersected the ramp down which Marguerite continued to move in the manner described, a combination of all three, which is to say, quite simply, that had he been able to inject sufficient force via his left and/or right foot/feet such that his centre of gravity would have advanced even marginally (he thought) beyond his left foot then this would have enabled him to launch his right foot, as he'd hoped to do, before his left foot had returned to ground, thereby saving himself precious seconds in his now pressing investigation into the disappearance of Harold Absalon, the Mayor's transport advisor, who remained missing and was presumed dead.

34

THE UNOCCUPIED SKATEBOARD freewheeled downhill, then, as the right foot commenced its hemicircle, as he had come to think of it in the interlude since the previous chapter, around his left leg, and this term 'hemicircle' and its use within the phrase 'as the right foot commenced its hemicircle, as he had come to think of it in the interlude since the previous chapter, around his left leg' was, of course, derived, as may be apparent to the more astute of those following in his footsteps, from the term 'hemisphere', and what he liked – indeed, loved – about this new usage (as he took it to be) was its allusion to the previous imagery of circumnavigation, bringing with it, he thought, the nautical, global connotations of adventures of no little risk, which he thought applied appropriately and fully, albeit in a less watery setting, to his own precarious situation. What he had stumbled upon, then, figuratively speaking, in this term 'hemicircle' and its use within the phrase 'as the right foot commenced its hemicircle, as he had come to think of it in the interlude since the previous chapter, around his left leg', was a continuation of imagery associated with the hazardous – sometimes deadly – nautical and global voyages that his forebears must have undertaken in whatever direction, from new to old world, or vice versa, in securing slaves, say, or having been enslaved. And the way in which this term 'hemicircle' and its use within the phrase 'as the right foot commenced its hemicircle, as he had come to think of it in the interlude since the previous chapter, around his left leg' was associated with such journeys was through its overlap, as it were, with the word hemisphere (which he took to be a more elegant way of referring to exactly half a sphere) and particularly in relation to 'the northern hemisphere' when contrasted with 'the southern hemisphere', with the aforementioned journeys involving the transition, by ship or other seagoing vessel, from the latter to the former (or vice versa, and perhaps back again on the other side of the sphere in what he thought was referred to as a circumnavigation of the globe, with the globe in question being, of course, the planet that he was then inhabiting and which he took it that most if not all of us continued to inhabit whilst apprehending, through whatever means ongoingly mysterious to him, his machinations on the topic of hemispheres, hemicircles and circumnavigations). He had, then, appropriated the first part of the word hemisphere and attached it to 'circle' to form what he thought was a new usage – 'hemicircle' – this to describe the trajectory that his right foot was currently engaged in around his left leg as fulcrum whilst the skateboard continued to freewheel, as it's known, unoccupied down the slope that he continued to move down in the manner described towards the horizontal rectangular plane that would also, he hoped, be the landing area for the woman in the tight-fitting pinstriped suit following her descent, in the usual fashion, down the steps leading to it from the right. And this neologism also pointed pleasingly, to his mind, towards both the familiar word 'semicircle' and, indeed, he now noticed, simply replaced the first letter of that word with a letter that was located earlier, temporally if not spatially, in the alphabet (at least within the alphabet that he was as it were employing to formulate his investigation; it may not, of course, be the language in which you are as it were accessing his investigation, in which case it would be for others to tamper, somehow, with this evidence, without his knowledge and certainly without changing the sense or substance of the conclusions of this branch of his investigation), thereby importing greater specificity in that, through its association with the term 'hemisphere', this being the other direction in which the neologism as it were pointed, one knew that his new term hemicircle related precisely to a half-circle, and more specifically still, to the circular part of the circumference of a half-circle that his right foot was as it were tracing around his left leg in its partial circumnavigation of that leg, with, as before, the association, in his mind at least, between the terms circumnavigation and hemisphere (particularly in its northern and southern aspects) adding a pleasing further resonance to his new term 'hemicircle'.

Granted that, strictly speaking, the correct term, he now realised, was, in fact 'semicircle' given that its meaning was indistinguishable from that of his new usage; yet he preferred the neologism, and would continue to use it simply because he took it to be clearer about the precise portion of the circle (i.e., a half) that he took his right foot to be traversing around his left leg whereas the prefix 'semi-' left the door open, as it were, to his mind, simply to be a part, and not necessarily a half (as in semi-skilled, semi-detached, semi-conscious etc.) of that circle, as in the previously cited partial circumambulation of right leg by left foot. On further reflection, though, he wondered whether 'hemicircle' and indeed the original 'hemisphere' is, and are, the correct terms for the location and actions in question. What he meant to say by this, as the woman in the tight-fitting pinstriped suit continued down the flight of stairs towards the horizontal rectangular plane that also formed the landing position for the ramp down which Marguerite continued to move, was that he wondered whether the hemicircle and hemisphere were, in fact, the correct shapes (one two-dimensional, of course, the other three-) to describe what he, and, in some cases relating in particular to the hemisphere, others, had used them to describe. After all, what he was wanting to describe at the moments when he used those terms were, he thought, in the first case a *uni*dimensional area (which is to say, a line) and in the second case a two-dimensional area (which is to say, a surface), albeit that, in both cases, the additional dimension was needed to describe these elements in space, given their curvature. The incorrect use of these terms, then, had resulted, he could say, in one additional dimension being in play, given that in using the term hemicircle, which he took to be a two-dimensional shape, he had, in fact, been hoping to describe a unidimensional (i.e. linear) shape and, similarly, in using the term hemi*sphere*, which he took to be a three-dimensional shape, he (and others, note) had, he thought, been hoping to describe a two-dimensional shape, again with the caveat relating to the requirement for the additional dimension for the purposes of description. In short, then, the volume implied by the term hemisphere should, he thought, more properly have been an area, or even more properly, a *surface* area as in the case of the southern hemisphere of, say, the planet that we are, presumably, collectively inhabiting, and the area implied by the term hemicircle should, more properly, he thought, be the hemi-circumference of the circle that his right foot would trace through the air around his left leg as he literally, metaphorically and figuratively took the next step in his investigation into the disappearance of Harold Absalon, the Mayor's transport advisor, whose forebears, he thought, originated, in fact, from both southern and northern climes, as he now chose to refer to them.

35

THE LEFT FOOT having come to ground then, with a thud, the right foot had now commenced what he had started referring to, remember, as a hemi-circumference of that left foot such that, at its completion, which is to say at the completion of that hemi-circumference traced by the right foot around the left, the feet, left and right, would be in their rightful places once again, viz: the right foot to the right of the left and, by extension, the left foot to the left of the right – this from Marguerite's perspective and from our own (assuming we, like the skateboard-owner, are following in Marguerite's footsteps from the rear). And it was for this reason, perhaps, that, in using the term 'rightful' in relation to the relative positions of the feet, which is to say in relation to the relationship between the feet at that future moment when the right foot would complete tracing its so-called hemi-circumference around its counterpart (the left foot), an equivalent term 'leftful' would not, in fact, be required. The point was, perhaps, sufficiently clear to all but the slowest of his investigative colleagues playing, as it did, upon different senses of the term 'right' that did not pertain, in fact, to its counterpart (in one of those senses), which was the left, yet he spelt it out nevertheless, so that all, regardless of investigative capability, could continue to follow the nuances of his investigation (etc.). The point related, then, to the fact that were the right foot to be to the right of the left foot – this from

Marguerite's perspective and from our own (assuming we, like the skateboard-owner, are following in Marguerite's footsteps from the rear) – a position that it would, in fact, attain having completed its hemi-circumference around same (for reasons he would no doubt come on to) then, by extension (and this meaning was contained within the words themselves rather than within external circumstances, although the latter must, in some still undefined way, somehow match the former), the left foot must, he thought, also be to the left of the right foot, again, of course, from Marguerite's perspective and from our own (etc.). In other words, in asserting that the rightful place for the right foot was to the right of its counterpart (the left foot) and that, by extension, when the right foot was in that rightful place to the right of the left foot the left foot must also be in its rightful place to the left of that right foot, a statement to that effect, viz, that the left foot was in its rightful place to the left of the right foot would, in fact, be tautological, he thought, meaning that it could, in fact, be inferred from the foregoing, which is to say that it could be inferred from the fact that the right foot was in its rightful place to the right of the left foot to the extent that it didn't really need to be made explicit in the way that he had been making it in the foregoing. Stating, then, quite simply, that the right foot was (or would shortly, we hope, be) in its rightful place to the right of the left foot was sufficient to imply, without stating it explicitly, that the left foot was also (or would shortly also be) in its rightful place – a different place, of course, from the right foot, in that the left foot's rightful place was, of course, to the left of that right foot from Marguerite's perspective, as before, and from our own (etc.). Given what one could, then, infer from the fact that the right foot would, once it had attained a geo-location to the right of the left foot, be in its rightful place in relation to that foot, which made stating that the left foot was also in its rightful place to the left of the right foot redundant, then it followed that having stated the former one did not necessarily need to state the latter, which is to say that one could simply state that the right foot was (or would be) in its rightful place to the right of the left foot from Marguerite's perspective, as before, and from our own (etc.) without stating that the converse was also the case, which is to say without stating that the left foot was also in *its* rightful place to the *left* of the right foot from the same perspective(s), and this non-statement had the added advantage (and this was the main point that he had set out, however imperfectly, to convey at the outset of this branch of his investigation) of not needing to append the word 'rightful' to the leftmost perambulant appendage, which helped avoid the urge that he, and perhaps others amongst us, had felt, momentarily, to retain the suffix whilst switching the adverb, given that, the non-word 'leftful' was, he felt, inadmissible since the adverb 'left-' did not contain the same alternative meanings as its counterpart 'right-', although it did, of course, contain a myriad of other, different, senses that he would not go into at that moment given that his right foot had, indeed, fully found its rightful place to the right of his left foot and that he could now hear footsteps directly behind him, originating, he presumed, from the erstwhile skateboarder rather than from ourselves (about whom Marguerite could, of course, have no easy conception in his ongoing investigation into the disappearance of Harold Absalon, the Mayor's transport advisor, who was missing presumed dead).

36

WHAT WAS HE to do now, he wondered, with his right foot in place, which is to say the right foot having landed on the inclined surface that was the ramp leading down to the horizontal rectangular plane? He was, in a sense, back where he began, in that his right foot was now to the right of his left foot, and vice versa (which is to say, for completeness, that his left foot was to the left of his right foot). And the parenthetical clarification was, on reflection, wholly justified, he thought, given, as before[23], the potential confusion between the variables, even if the range of potential values of these variables was limited – in fact it was limited to two values, each of which could be taken to be the opposite of the other, in that these two values were 'left' and 'right'. So the field of values was a set consisting of no more than and no less than two, which was to say that that field consisted of precisely two values: the value (if that was what it was) 'left' and the value (etc.) 'right'. It was not, then, the set of values that was the complicating factor in determining what he should do next, as he noticed that the woman in the tight-fitting pinstriped suit had started to scrutinise him and his actions in a way that was hitherto unthinkable, as she continued down the flight of stairs towards the horizontal rectangular plane that

23 Instead of a place of assignation, I'd been ejected through a side exit into a refuse area, a ramp and stairs leading up from it to street level. And I was not alone within that space.

also formed the landing position for the ramp down which Marguerite hoped to continue shortly to descend. Instead it must be the complexity of the function into which these variables must, as it were, be plugged in the situation he found himself unable to proceed within, which is to say, a situation in which his right foot had landed on the downwardly inclined slope that intersected the horizontal rectangular plane towards which the woman in the tight-fitting pinstriped suit was also gravitating, and, having landed, left him, given the complexity, not really quite knowing how to proceed further both physically and in his investigation into the disappearance of Harold Absalon, the Mayor's transport advisor, who was missing presumed dead. Unfortunately the situation was, in fact, more complex than even he had imagined given that his right foot was, in fact, in advance, now, of his left, since, as we know, it had completed its partial circumnavigation of the latter by tracing the curved part at the perimeter of what he had originally termed a hemicircle and now referred to as a hemi-circumference, with the majority of that curved part located mostly to the right of that left foot and centred upon the centre of it, a distinction, this, that he felt he should have made earlier. What this meant was that there was at least one further variable in play, as it were, a variable that could be assigned one of two opposing values, but values that were, in fact, different to the previously identified values of 'left' and 'right', and these values were, of course, the aforementioned 'in front of' and 'behind'[24]. The situation he found himself in, then, was one of stasis or near-stasis given that the functional

24 He was going through the wheelie bins and had his back to me, but I could tell he was wearing clothes that were identical to my own, down to the jacket's leather elbow patches.

relationship appeared to be too complex for even his exceptional investigative mind to compute, one in which there was a series of binary variables relating to foot-identity (left or right), lateral position (to the left or to the right of) and longitudinal position (in front of or behind), with the field of values for each of those variables consisting of: left foot (L) and right (Γ); to the left (<) or to the right (>) of; and in front of (Λ) or behind (V). Upon still further reflection, however, Marguerite realised that this was not, in fact, the end of the complexity that he (or his feet) found himself (or themselves) in given that he was on a decline, remember, suggesting that when one of his feet was in front of or behind the other then it must, *ipso facto*, also be below or above that other foot, respectively, as in the current scenario, which yields the following: above (A) or below (V). Tempted as he was to set out the interdependencies between these values and variables as a way out of this impasse (e.g. given the fact that if the right foot is to the right of, and in front of, the left foot, as in the current scenario, it follows that the left foot is: to the left of; behind; and above the right foot, which might look something like this: $\Gamma>L+\Gamma\Lambda L\equiv L<\Gamma+LV\Gamma+LA\Gamma$) he decided, instead, to dramatically reduce the number of variables as an aid to decision-making and to the prompt recommencement of his investigation into the disappearance of Harold Absalon, the Mayor's transport advisor, who was missing presumed dead. And the way in which he would do this this was by simply bringing his left foot to rest alongside his right. At a stroke, then, he would rule as inadmissible any but the most basic propositional determinants, and, in so doing, would surely render the means by which he would continue to unearth the circumstances of the disappearance of Harold Absalon adequately clear even to the rawest of raw recruits. It was in this way, then, that he would decisively move forward at least one stage in his investigation as, lifting the heel of his left foot from the decline upon which it had hitherto been resting – an action he accomplished by moving his centre of gravity forwards slightly and increasing the angle subtended between his left shin and the top of his left foot – he commenced the action of moving that foot through a flat parabola whose shape would, he hoped, result, before too long, in that left foot coming to rest alongside and, simply, to the left of, its pedicurial counterpart.

37

I T W A S I N this way, then, that he would bring his left foot
to rest alongside his right, which is to say, as uttered, *sotto
voce*, numerous times, to rest to the left of that right foot; and
the manner in which it would come to rest, he thought, having
completed the aforementioned flat parabola, if that is not a
contradiction in terms, was by initially placing the left heel
alongside its counterpart, which is to say alongside the heel of
the right foot; the left heel, having been the first part of that
foot that had as it were taken to the air in literally taking this
step, it followed, in some fashion, that it would be the first part
of that foot that would come to ground again, particularly given
the nature of the incline towards which it was headed. In other
words, given that the ground as it were fell away, in that he was
moving down a decline, rather than moving up an incline, it
followed, he thought, that it would be the heel of his left foot
that would first make contact with that decline following the
termination of the passage of that foot through the air. Yet this
was not predetermined by the parameters of the situation he
found himself in, he thought, as he noticed that the breath of
the woman in the tight-fitting pinstriped suit had shortened
and become more laboured, as evidenced by the movements of
the waistband at the top of the skirt that formed part of that
tight-fitting suit. Granted, the point about the falling away of
the landform, to call it that, was, or might be, a valid one to
make, as the ball of his left foot left that decline, following the

lead set by the heel of the same foot; after all, were he to be *a*scending an *in*cline (and he wondered whether also to italicise the 'n' in 'an', given that the 'an' only applied to the incline and would not, in this language, apply also to the *de*cline, where an unitalicised (or a non-italicised) 'a' would be the order of the day; but he decided against it for reasons that, for some reason, remain inaccessible to us) then it might follow that the ball or even the toes of that foot would, in fact, encounter that landform prior to the equivalent heel making contact with same; and the reason for this would be the fact that, in the situation where he was walking up an incline, particularly a steep one, then the ground would, as it were, be rising up to meet that approaching foot; to give the extreme example: were he to be approach what's known as a sheer incline (which is to say, the counterpart of the sheer drop) such as the wall directly ahead of him on the other side of the horizontal rectangular plane then it would be the toes that make contact with this incline, and the fronts of the toes in particular, rather than the ball or the heel or any other part of the equivalent foot (the left, in the situation that he actually found himself in). The toes would be leading in that situation in relation to the precipitous incline, and it would be for that reason that these parts of that foot would as it were touch down upon that surface (although, of course, in the case of the extreme situation that he was sketching it would not be a downwards movement given that surface would be in front of those parts of the foot that would make contact with it, in which case it might be better to say that those toes would, yes, simply be the first portion of that foot to make contact with that surface). Now, the toes were, in fact, also leading in the situation that Marguerite found himself in, a situation, remember, in which the ball of the left foot had just left the decline down which he continued to travel, the heel of that foot having left that surface some moments previously. The question, then, remained: why did he think that it would be the heel of that foot that would be the first part of same to touch down (an appropriate term here, for what he hoped were obvious reasons) upon that decline – clearly he didn't feel he could simply rely on the fact that the reason that the heel of that foot would be the first to touch down was that that part of his anatomy (and, more specifically, that part of that part of his anatomy) had been the first, on that side (the left) to have become airborne in making the transition from being above, behind and to the left of the opposing foot (the right); no, he felt, as the whole of that foot now started to move through the air, that he needed to ground his justifications in something much less speculative than that.

And he felt that the extreme example did, in fact, offer a way of resolving the conundrum that was facing him. After all, from the point of view of the decline (and he eschewed italicisation for the duration of that word, despite it being in counter-distinction to that angle of the surface in the *in extremis* example) it could be argued that his heel would (or could, at least) be in the lead, in relation to the other parts of that foot (the left) in that, by the time that foot had revolved in its passage towards its landing point adjacent to, and to the left of, the right foot, then the heel could, in the crucial moments before touch down, be the part of that part of his anatomy (the left foot) that was closest to that surface. But didn't this new formulation simply beg the question, he wondered, as, momentarily, he lost his train of thought[25], as it's

25 Intent on examining an item he'd retrieved from the bin in front of him, he seemed not to notice me.

known? Isn't this just a restatement of his contention that the left heel, having led the way in taking off from the surface, would also lead the way in terms of touchdown in the previously identified location? He thought it was, essentially, but that this reformulation had, at least, added the revolutionary element, which is to say that it had indicated that the foot, in moving through the air would, and was, note, revolving around the ankle, which is to say that the toes were moving upwards with the remainder of that foot around the axis formed by the left ankle, a revolution that, were it to continue on the same angular trajectory, would have the effect, in essence, of moving those toes, and the ball of the same foot, away from the decline down which Marguerite continued, in this fashion, to descend and, in so doing, would render those parts of that part of his anatomy (which is to say, his left foot) effectively inadmissible as left-sided touchdown trailblazers, an accolade that would as it were fall to the heel of the same foot. How, though, did he know that his left foot would, in fact, revolve sufficiently in the manner described such that it would render the aforementioned parts of that part of his anatomy ineligible for the identified accolade, if, after all, that was what it was? And the answer was that he did not know this. It depended, again, on so many variables – the extent to which the remainder of his anatomy had revolved, and was revolving, around his *right* ankle, which is to say the extent that he was leaning forwards in his ongoing passage down that decline; the speed of his descent; the angular velocity of revolution of that left foot; and so on – and he seemed increasingly incapable of computing such complexity, despite his renown in this area, a renown that he thought was justified given his previous accomplishments as an investigator. Instead, then, he resolved simply to see what happened following the passage of his left foot through the air towards his right foot. He would, as it were, sit, perhaps like us, and wait.

And what he found, as the woman in the tight-fitting pin-striped suit appeared, now, somehow, directly before him with a look of anguished concern on her face, was that his left heel did not, in fact, make the initial contact alongside his right; nor, in fact did the toes or the ball of that left foot make the aforementioned initial contact; it was, in fact, his left foot, *in its entirety* (which is to say, including the tacitly discounted arch of that foot), which touched down, as it were simultaneously on that decline. And he realised, as he slumped into the arms, as it's known, of that woman, and she embraced him if not passionately then, at least, earnestly, that the angle of that foot must have precisely matched the angle subtended, to the vertical, by the decline at the moment of touchdown and, furthermore, that he must be what's known as flatfooted, which is, or was, in fact, the case.

38

H E WONDERED HOW he had ended up like this, which is to say how he had ended up in the arms of the woman in the tight-fitting pinstriped suit, the briefcase, the skateboard and its owner now nowhere to be seen. He also wondered whether, in fact, this was how he had ended up, or would end up, which is to say, in different, hopefully definitively, now, clear words, whether this was the end for him, or the end of this particular investigation, or of this particular branch of his investigation, rather than the end of him *per se*, which is to say the end of his life on earth, that, presumably, being the planet upon which all this action, so-called, is taking, and has taken, place. In still other words, was him ending up in the arms, as it's known, of the woman in the tight-fitting pinstriped suit actually the end of this particular investigation, as, presumably, is being suggested by the sparseness (if that's the right word) or rather the fewness (would be better) of the remaining pages of this particular thin volume? It could not be ruled out, of course, that he may not remain in those arms at the point right at the end of this thin volume, and, were this to be the case then it could be said that that was not, in fact, how he had ended up in that him being in the arms of the woman in the tight-fitting pinstriped suit had been something that had taken place before the action had as it were come to a close, which is to say that she – the woman in the tight-fitting pinstriped suit – having taken him into her arms, as it is still known, had not continued to keep him in those arms beyond the point at which we are no longer able to see him[26], which would mean that this, which is to say the being in the arms of the woman in the tight-fitting pinstriped suit, was not, in fact, how he had ended up, unless, of course, the missing skateboarder had, as it were and literally, stuck a dagger in him with their favoured hand, which is to say had stuck a blade into his back as a means of bringing his life to an end. And in this latter scenario, the one involving the missing skateboarder sticking a dagger or other sharp blade into Marguerite's back as a way of ending the latter's life then it could, of course, be said that this was, indeed, in a definitive way now, how it had ended up for our detective in that, regardless of whether this particular thin volume was seemingly or actually coming to an end, as indicated to us if not to him, by the number of remaining pages, his life would be at an end suggesting that, were the woman in the tight-fitting pinstriped suit to keep Marguerite in her arms, as it's known, during what are known, he thought, as the death throes, then this might be how things would end up for him even if he were not still in her arms at the end of this thin volume. Given the fact, though, that he still continued to function cognitively at a reasonably advanced level; that his body remained more or less upright, albeit supported by the arms of the woman in the tight-fitting pinstriped suit; and, most importantly, that he no longer felt any physical aches or pains whatsoever, then he thought and hoped that this was not, in fact, how he had ended up or would end up, assuming these to be necessary

26 I resolved finally to speak, but the words froze in my throat: Harold Absalon had turned to face me.

and sufficient conditions for ruling out such an eventuality.

In what way, given the foregoing, could it be said, then, that that was how he had ended up, which is to say, in the arms, as it is known, of the woman in the tight-fitting pinstriped suit? Given he would not countenance the idea that this was a definitive termination in the sense of the end of his life through murderous action towards him by the missing skateboarder, whether entirely gratuitously or on behalf, perhaps, of Richard Knox, a colleague, remember, of Harold Absalon's with whom the Mayor's transport advisor had fallen out, as it's known, just prior to his disappearance, and that he was not, yet, willing to assert that he would remain in the arms, as it is known, of the woman in the tight-fitting pinstriped suit at the close of this particular thin volume (in part because he could have no conception of volumes and their close given the fact that what is taking place for him is as real, for him, as our experience is real for us), then in what sense could it be said that this was how he had ended up? Was he simply enquiring, by wondering how he had ended up like this, about the conditions that must have been in place for him to be in the embrace, to call it that now, of the woman in the tight-fitting pinstriped suit, which is to say, enquiring as to how it had come to pass that he was in the arms of the woman in question, with the expression 'had come to pass' being indicative of the fact that he may not always remain in those arms, which is to say that he may be released from them before this thin volume, in whatever way ongoingly mysterious to him, is brought to a close, without undermining this very enquiry into how he had ended up like this, which is to say how he had ended up in the arms of the woman in the tight-fitting pinstriped suit? Perhaps, in other words, he was using the phrases 'ending up like this' and 'coming to pass' synonymously, with his primary interest being in the circumstances that had brought that still ongoing physical intimacy into existence; but what was perplexing him (and, no doubt, the more astute of those of us who are, or were, following in his investigative, which is to say, his inquisitive footsteps, as it were) was the fact that he had used all of this thin volume up until the point of actually being in the arms of the woman in the tight-fitting pinstriped suit describing how he now found himself in those arms. In what sense, then, could he be interested, now, in identifying those circumstances given the very full and detailed account that he had already provided of them? Or was the implication that there were circumstances that were quite other to those that he had been at such pains to provide an account of that were responsible for him ending up (in the sense, of course, that he is still in the process of explicating) in the way that he had ended up (etc.), which is to say in the arms of the woman in the tight-fitting pinstriped suit? If those circumstances were not, in fact, quite other, which is to say, were not parallel to and distinct from those that he had provided an account of, then was he saying (or wondering, aloud, as it were, rather) that there were, perhaps, one or more hidden, as it were, circumstances that are, or is, necessary to provide a full account of him being (still, note) in the arms, as it is known, of the woman in the tight-fitting pinstriped suit? In other words was he, and had he been, all along, placing the emphasis on the wondering, which is to say on the hitherto obscure circumstance(s) that had brought the embrace about, to refer to it in that way now, rather than on the sense of him ending up like that? It could not be ruled out, given that he was the one, of course, doing the wondering whilst also being the one who had provided this account to us in the first place. The sense, then, was, perhaps, that the embrace of him by the woman in the tight-fitting pinstriped suit was, in fact, ultimately unexpected – by him, if not by us – and it was this that had got him wondering about what had, in fact, occasioned or precipitated it. It was this sense that he, in turn, embraced, which is to say that he confirmed that this was, in fact, what he had meant when he had wondered, to himself, presumably, rather than aloud, how he had ended up like this, which is to say in the arms, as it is known, of the woman in the tight-fitting pinstriped suit, meaning that he had simply been wondering about her motivation for taking him into her arms in this way regardless of whether or not he ended up like this in another sense, such as this being the arrangement between them right up to the end of the current thin volume, or of his life, or of life itself, although, given how elated he felt at this physical intimacy with her (to the extent that he could feel the contours of the front of her body in relation to the changing contours of the front of his own) he did wish that this embrace, which was something he had sought for so long – and which had been in such jeopardy – would, in fact, continue indefinitely in the sense of it, rather than the description of it, being open-ended, which is to say, without end, at least without an end that we can see beyond the end.

ACKNOWLEDGEMENTS

THANKS SO MUCH to Jen and Chris Hamilton-Emery for your belief, boldness and support. Thanks to Nicholas Royle for your perseverance in the face of endlessly proliferating clauses. And to Danayutta for your patience and guidance: heartfelt thanks, and love.

NEW FICTION FROM SALT

ELEANOR ANSTRUTHER
A Perfect Explanation (978-1-78463-164-2)

NEIL CAMPBELL
Lanyards (978-1-78463-170-3)

MARK CAREW
Magnus (978-1-78463-204-5)

ANDREW COWAN
Your Fault (978-1-78463-180-2)

AMANTHI HARRIS
Beautiful Place (978-1-78463-193-2)

S. A. HARRIS
Haverscroft (978-1-78463-200-7)

CHRISTINA JAMES
Chasing Hares (978-1-78463-189-5)

NEW FICTION FROM SALT

NEW POETRY FROM SALT

AMIT CHAUDHURI
Sweet Shop (978-1-78463-182-6)

DAVID BRIGGS
Cracked Skull Cinema (978-1-78463-207-6)

PETER DANIELS
My Tin Watermelon (978-1-78463-209-0)

MATTHEW HAIGH
Death Magazine (978-1-78463-206-9)

ANDREW McDONNELL
The Somnambulist Cookbook (978-1-78463-199-4)

ELEANOR REES
The Well at Winter Solstice (978-1-78463-184-0)

TONY WILLIAMS
Hawthorn City (978-1-78463-212-0)

This book has been typeset by
SALT PUBLISHING LIMITED
using Neacademia, a font designed by Sergei Egorov
for the Rosetta Type Foundry in the Czech Republic. It
is manufactured using Holmen Book Cream 70gsm, a
Forest Stewardship Council™ certified paper from the
Hallsta Paper Mill in Sweden. It was printed and bound
by Clays Limited in Bungay, Suffolk, Great Britain.

CROMER
GREAT BRITAIN
MMXX